Daughter of Madrugada

Also by Frances M. Wood

Becoming Rosemary

Daughter of

Madrugada

FRANCES M. WOOD

Delacorte Press

Published by
Delacorte Press
an imprint of
Random House Children's Books
a division of Random House, Inc.
1540 Broadway
New York, New York 10036

Visit us on the Web! www.randomhouse.com/kids
Educators and librarians, for a variety of teaching tools, visit us at
www.randomhouse.com/teachers

Cataloging-in-Publication Data is available from the
Library of Congress.
ISBN 0-385-32719-6 (trade)
ISBN 0-385-90038-4 (lib. bdg.)

The text of this book is set in 12-point Galliard.

Book design by Patrice Sheridan

Manufactured in the United States of America

May 2002

10 9 8 7 6 5 4 3 2 1

BVG

Para las niñas de mi familia—
Lesley, Alyson, Kumari, Anneke,
y Laura Jane

Con gratitud al
North Carolina Arts Council
por su apoyo financiero

Y con mil gracias al
Señor Edward Wood,
al Señor Eduardo Perez,
a la Señora Melissa Chiti,
y como siempre,
a BJM

And a special thanks to my editor,
Jennifer Wingertzahn,
who kept on saying,
"Think in English!"

Contents

	A Note from the Author	ix
1.	The Wind	1
2.	American Spies	2
3.	We Have Lost the War	7
4.	*Madrugada* Means Dawn	17
5.	A Real American	28
6.	Hortencia Goes Hunting	40
7.	Penance	53
8.	Californio Women	59
9.	The River	69
10.	The Dennys and the Dons	79
11.	At School with Padre Mournful	89
12.	The Doña of the Mill	95
13.	Mrs. Denny's Pies	108
14.	Uncle Sam Is Rich Enough	120
15.	The Fence	130
16.	*Fuego*	138
17.	The *San Judás Tadeo*	146
18.	Listen, Wind!	155
	A Historical Note	160

A Note from the Author

Discúlpenme ustedes, por favor . . .

. . . for my (I hope creative) misuse of the Spanish language. Even now I can hear my mother—a *frontera* girl from Arizona/Sonora—fiercely saying, *"La Madrugada,"* correcting my ever-Americanized version of her native tongue. So I know better: Cesa's ranch should be called El Rancho de la Madrugada. But the *gringa* half of my mind takes shortcuts, drops articles. And there you have it. Not exactly Spanglish, but something close.

So forgive me, please, for being a granddaughter of Mexico who takes liberties with the language. It's how I think, it's how I dream—in a *mezcla* of words and languages.

FRANCES M. WOOD

ix

Chapter 1

The Wind

Listen, Wind! Do you hear me? Your gusts are wet and salty—they feel so strange upon my face and hands. Nothing like the sweet breezes I used to know, filled with chaparral and oak and wild grasses. O Wind, change direction and take me home. Take me back to Rancho Madrugada. . . .

Chapter 2

American Spies

I've always talked to the wind, but it used to be a game. Like the game that I played with my brothers late last winter, almost a year ago. Dos, Tres and I were out searching for spies. We were riding horses along a ridgeline high above, but still within, our California ranch. Rancho Madrugada.

I stopped, surprising all of our horses. "O Wind!" I implored.

"What, Cesa?" my second brother, Dos, asked me.

I hadn't spoken to him; Dos isn't always too bright. "Hush!" I commanded.

Dos stilled his pony with a touch to its neck.

"O Wind!" The breeze blew from the west that day. I remember that, so clearly. Because there was the smallest hint of salt in the air. "Bring us a spy!"

It was more than a request. It was a demand. Ever since war was declared between Mexico and the United States in 1846 we de Haro children had been hunting for enemies. Americans. But we hadn't seen even one yet. Probably because all the real fighting was so far away from our home. Probably because most of the fighting had stopped. But I hoped. We all hoped. There was always a chance.

Dos was ten then. My third brother, Tres, was nine. I, at thirteen, was their leader. I pushed back my hair—too long for a general of the Mexican army, but long enough for a Mexican girl—and turned my nose again to the wind.

"Cesa!" Tres let his horse circle around me, then dance a little. He waved one of his arms.

I teased Tres by not responding. Instead I breathed in, smelling deeply, tasting the richness of the high meadows, crushed by rain and now reborn. The truth was, we de Haros hadn't seen even an innocent American, a neutral—a merchant ship captain—since the fighting began.

"*Cesa!*" Tres insisted.

"Oh, all right." I peered in the direction he was indicating.

"See?" Tres said tantalizingly.

I saw. A figure on horseback, galloping wildly in the valley below. I considered.

"He's very tall!" I finally said, making Tres grin.

"He sits his horse very badly!" Dos chimed in.

"His beard is very long!" Tres exulted.

"He's an American spy!" I shouted.

With whoops of war we spurred our horses down the green, grassy slopes. Still yelling, we rode behind and up to the eldest of my brothers, Grego. Who is neither tall, a bad rider nor bearded. Most certainly, Grego isn't bearded.

"Halt!" I commanded.

"Shoot him!" Dos screamed.

Grego glared at us, but in the wrong way. I saw, then Dos and Tres saw, that Grego wasn't willing to play along. But still, we pursued him. "Stop in the name of the Republic of Mexico!"

"No!" Grego's voice was as loud as ours were, but more angry, determined. "Look!" He didn't slow down. He made us race beside him. I looked, and the others did, too. But all we saw was something like a bowl—maybe it was a stiff and flattened bag—attached to Grego's arm by a leather strap. I tried to match Grego's rhythm so that I could see better. Our horses loped along as though they were matching waves.

"A hat?" I asked.

"An American hat!" Grego declared.

My stomach jolted. The hat of an enemy! I, too, leaned over my horse's neck. We rode for home with dire intensity.

At the house, we four slid off our horses, all talking, all shouting. Now I could see enough of the hat to realize it was a dark blue cap with a leather shade over the eyes. American, for sure. "Spy!"

"Hush!" Our great-aunt—dressed in black, forever a widow—stepped from the parlor onto the veranda and waved us to silence. "Enough!"

"Tía!" I dropped my reins and began to explain. After all, I was the oldest, it was my place to speak first.

But Grego hopped onto the veranda. He pushed his words in front of mine. "Tía!" He showed her the hat.

Tía took the hat from Grego. She studied it. And then she sighed. She didn't call for help—one of the servants to run for Grandfather and Papi, another servant to round up those men working closest to the house. Instead she brushed the hat off—as if that could make it clean! "Your uncle Isidro returned this morning," she told us. "He is resting. Be as quiet as possible. Wash and change, and then come to the table for the noon meal."

Had our aunt lost her mind? I was on the veranda now, too, and I stepped in front of Grego. "We must do something, Tía!" I tried to make my voice stern, adult. I stood almost as tall as my aunt. I could make my back equally rigid—although I was shaking, just a little.

"I don't know where the American is now," Grego warned. "I found the hat way south, beside the creek, near the path that leads to San José."

We stood like a small army before our aunt, our

hearts racing, waiting for her to call the alarm so that we could jump onto our horses and race again.

But: "Your uncle met the man." Tía was so calm, her words so measured. "He was an American, as you say. But no danger to us. He was only passing through an edge of our ranch and is probably long gone by now. So go wash, children, and prepare for dinner."

"He might be a spy, Tía!" I said.

"We're at war!" my brothers clamored.

"Hush!" Again Tía silenced us. "Your uncle is resting."

We hushed our voices. But we had to move. Our hands and legs were as restless as our hearts. Grego elbowed Dos. Tres kicked at the veranda floor.

"Children!" Tía reached to quiet us with her hands: a grip upon Grego's shoulder, a firm palm upon my back. "There are no spies. Not any longer. Your uncle came home from Mexico City with official word. The war with the United States is over."

"Hurray!" my brothers exploded.

This time Tía only shook her head. "Go wash," she said.

Chapter 3

We Have Lost the War

At meals we sit in order of precedence, which means that Grandfather sits in his great chair at the high end of the table with Papi and Uncle Isidro right beside him. Tía and we children cluster around the other end of the table. When Grego turned twelve, he got to move up and sit next to Papi, like a man. Even though he is a whole year younger than me. I still haven't quite forgiven Grego for that.

On the day that we learned the war had ended, Grego took the seat next to Uncle Isidro, because that was where the news was. I had to observe our uncle from a distance. Uncle Isidro is years younger than Papi, but on this day he looked older. Much older. And weary. But then, he'd been traveling, away from the ranch for months.

We waited in silence while the servants brought the food. It was Lent, the season of loss and redemption, so we ate no meat. But we didn't starve. There were platters of chilies stuffed with cheese and eggs, and bowls of beans and minced green squash. Tortillas, of course, made of corn and wheat. And a whole dried salmon almost the size of my smallest brother, Cinco.

The servants stood with their hands clasped and their heads lowered for the blessing; with no priest with us that day, Grandfather spoke the words of thanks. Then Tía dismissed the servants. We all waited for Grandfather to pick up his fork.

"So." Grandfather was not only the first to eat, he was also, as always, the first to speak. "We have lost the war."

"Lost?" I squeaked. Tía frowned at me. Meals are not a time when children speak.

But how could we, the stalwart Mexicans of California, have lost the war? We were hidalgos, lords of the land. The Americans were tradesmen and sailors. They were nothing, nothing to us!

The men ignored my squeak. They spoke only amongst themselves. "So Upper California has been ceded to the United States," my father mused.

We had not only lost the war, we had lost our country? Did that mean our ranch, our land, was now part of America? I felt as though the ground moved, shifted—as it does during an earthquake. But there was no earthquake, only adult voices.

8

"The treaty is generous, sir." Uncle Isidro had turned toward Grandfather, and he spoke so courteously, and in a manner so cautious, he could have been addressing the king of Spain, not his own father. "We are guaranteed our freedoms, our property. We may choose to become Americans or retain our Mexican citizenship."

"American citizens!" Grandfather's face darkened dangerously. "Bah!"

"The treaty is generous," Uncle Isidro continued. "But . . ."

"But?" Papi encouraged.

"The treaty is meant to be interpreted in American courts. And American law is different from ours."

"Bah!" This time Grandfather slapped both hands down upon the table. His plate jumped. I jumped a little, too. Papi's wineglass toppled over.

"We de Haros are not American," Grandfather said with all the strength and will of a king. "Our ranch is not American soil. Despite any agreements made in Mexico City, *our lives will not change.*"

Papi and Uncle Isidro glanced at each other, as if disbelieving. But I nodded. I didn't understand about laws and courts and citizenship. But I knew my grandfather. He is indeed a king—the king of our ranch. And if he said that our lives will not change, then that was how things would be. The war had hardly touched us; what did its ending matter? Our lives would continue as always. Grandfather said so.

Beneath my chair, the world was blessedly solid again.

Cinco, six years old, yawned. Tired, and maybe even bored. He must have understood even less than I did, probably didn't even know what a treaty was. Cuatro, who was almost eight, yawned, too.

Tía, observing the little boys, rose. In her own way, Tía can be as much a queen as Grandfather is a king. "We will leave you men," she said. "Come, children." With her black skirts flowing, she swept out of the dining room followed by Dos, Tres, Cuatro and Cinco. My younger brothers have real names, too, but after Grego there came so many of them that we began calling them by numbers—Two, Three, Four and Five.

I lingered because Grego was staying with the men. He didn't even stand from his chair. He looked to make sure that I noticed—and then he turned his head back to listen soberly, gravely, to Uncle Isidro describe his months in Mexico City.

"Cesa!" said Tía.

I turned my back on Grego and, like Tía, swept out of the dining room and into the open corridor that surrounds our courtyard. Someday I, too, will be a queen. And I will not wear black. Tía shepherded the little boys into the room that they share with Grego; I began to daydream.

"Siesta, Cesa," Tía instructed.

But I was imagining a sun-yellow gown so full and

wide that it touched the whitewashed adobe wall of the house on one side of the corridor and dipped into the green and flowered courtyard on the other. My imaginary gown was woven with gold thread, overlaid with silver net. My imaginary slippers, upon the very real tile floor, were embroidered white and yellow. I nodded graciously to those servants who stood beneath the roofed shade of the corridor. I lifted my hand to salute the camellias enjoying the sun of the courtyard. Sunlight caught me, too, and I shone and sparkled all the way to my bedroom.

There darkness enclosed me and my finery disappeared into shadows. I took off the plain blue muslin petticoat that I had put on for dinner—which didn't even touch the floor, much less the walls. Finally obedient to Tía, I lay down upon my bed. I slept.

I dreamt: "Cesa." In my sleep I heard my name. "Cesa," said my father, and I knew that for him my name was short for *princesa,* and that I was his only princess. A princess, but with bones and brains as good as any boy's—that's what Papi always said. "Cesa!" said Tía, and I knew that for her my name was the same as the Spanish command to stop. "Stop!" Grego shouted—because I was bigger and stronger and could ride a horse faster. And then the voice that I always longed to hear, a voice that spoke softly, gently, lovingly. "María Francisca . . ." Which is my real name, my baptismal name.

I woke up. My cheeks were wet. And my mind was

11

holding, holding on to the sound of that voice. A voice that I only heard in my dreams; my mother's voice as it was before she became so ill with the fever, before she died.

"Mamá!" I whispered, still trying to hear.

But in only moments I lost it: Mamá's voice, that sweet memory. Just as I had lost Mamá. That had been a terrible time, when the world shifted in a horrible way and stayed broken and awry forever. With Mamá gone, everything changed. Everything we saw, everything we did, every moment of our lives.

I was eight then. I made Tía sew me my first pair of pantaloons so that I could follow along behind my grandfather and father. So that I could race ahead of my brothers. So that I would never be left behind again. And I wasn't. But still, I miss her so much.

I sat up to look out the window. Our walls are so thick that only a few rays of sunshine were working their way indoors; outside was a bright, bright glare. My pantaloons lay across a chair: rough-woven brown cloth, just like the men wear. I rose to peer into my mirror. My chemise was very fine, made of delicate lawn with lace sleeves. My pantaloons were practical, my chemise lovely. I wiped away the last of my tears and tied my hair back into a wide bow of black velvet.

I opened my door, bringing in the light of the corridor. I tiptoed across the courtyard and through the narrow, unroofed passageway between kitchen and parlor. There were sounds of movement, of life, inside

12

the kitchen, but all the way around to the west side of the house, I found only silence.

Our male house servants, as always, took their siesta upon the veranda—it entirely rims that side of the house. Some slept on the carved wooden benches, stretched out as if on beds. Others sat side by side, one's head on another's shoulder, one's arms dangling across another's knees. The little water boy—who spends his life carrying water from the creek to the kitchen barrel—slept sprawled upon the wooden veranda floor as if he would never awaken again.

I walked quietly, very quietly: not onto the veranda, but onto the hard-packed earth that is our western yard. I stopped, turned and made a circle. As I turned, I saw. And as I saw, my spirits rose. I lifted my arms until I was a spinning top. I exulted: Everything around me was ours. Everything belonged to the de Haro family. The horses in the corral, the long, low house, land almost as far as I could imagine. *Land.* That was Grandfather's voice inside my head, saying what he had said so often: *We de Haros would be nothing without our land.*

Our land, now so sweet and green and rich and beautiful after the long winter rains. I leaned against a madrone tree, red-barked and white-blossomed, to rest my spinning head, to smell the honeylike flowers.

But I couldn't rest. No one could. My four youngest brothers ran out onto the veranda like wild and howling Indians. Siesta was over. The real Indians, our servants, stirred and yawned and stood to resume their tasks of the day. The real Indians had work to do. They ignored us.

"Cesa!" Grego's call certainly meant "Stop!" He followed the smaller boys, but when they jumped down to the yard, Grego retained his dignity and descended the steps.

I narrowed my eyes. Grego was wearing the American hat pulled low over his ears and strapped beneath his chin. He looked both strange and ridiculous; he made a very short American. "I challenge you, Cesa!"

"War?" Dos suggested happily.

"Yes!" Cuatro was eager.

"Do we have to?" Cinco was not.

I was ready. I tore the bow from my hair and threw it at Grego's feet. "A challenge," I agreed. I knew what he was: "American interloper!"

"Mexican provoker," Grego retorted. He worked my ribbon into the dirt with the toe of his shoe.

We divided into two armies, just as we had been doing ever since the start of the real war. This time Grego was general to Tres, who is very bright if not very big, and Cuatro, who is always brave. I led Dos, more muscles than brains, and almost useless Cinco. Dos ran for the rifles of oak and swords of madrone that we keep stored beneath the veranda. Cinco walked resignedly toward the corral. Tres and Cuatro

14

were there before him, of course, grabbing the leading ropes of the fastest ponies.

I made my assessment. The enemy would have the advantage unless their general chose to ride with full saddle. Which he often did. Grego likes to be outfitted and spurred as gorgeously as possible. Especially when he is a general; especially when he is at war. Grego is very vain.

I had the advantage of his vanity.

"No saddles," I told my men. "Bareback!" And we threw ourselves upon the ponies that Cinco brought from the corral. We turned our noses, human and equine, toward the enemy.

"Zas!" Dos struck his sword sharply upon Grego's back. "You're dead!" Dos crowed.

"I'm resurrected," Grego snarled. Which is how we play: We die, then resurrect so that we don't run out of soldiers.

We clattered and banged until our ponies were huffing and Cinco pleaded, "Can we stop now?" Then we took stock.

"Seventeen of your men are dead, Cesa," Grego said with great satisfaction. "And only ten of mine." He smiled the smile that I hate the most, the one that says, *You may be the oldest, but I'm a boy.*

"You Mexicans have lost the war!" Cuatro gloated. "That's what Grandfather said."

"No!" I surprised even myself with my vehemence.

I grabbed the hat from Grego's head; I ground it into the dust. "American!" I spat as if it were a word that even a priest should not say out loud. "I have not lost. You have not lost. We have not lost!"

My brothers fell silent.

"You're not making any sense," Tres ventured.

But I knew what I was saying, I knew what was true. "Our lives will not change." I also quoted Grandfather, but I quoted him correctly. "Our lives will not change. Never again."

Chapter 4

Madrugada Means Dawn

Every morning just before dawn—before even a hint of daylight enters my room—Tía leaves her bed to stand in the corridor outside her own door and sing a hymn of praise. I hardly remember a day that hasn't started with the sound of Tía's voice rising high with the words "Now comes the dawn!" And by the time I have stumbled out of my bed and to my doorway, I can see the faint brightening over the top of the kitchen, the pale colors that soften the tops of the eastern hills. Still singing—we all sing, even Grandfather, even the little water boy—I cross back through my room to my west-facing window and wait. I don't have to wait long. "Light of the sky! God's gift to mankind," we all sing. And the western hills begin to glow, slowly at first, with tentative reaches of the awakening sun, until they blaze into color: hills of winter green surrounded by halos of gold.

The name of our ranch is El Rancho del Valle de la Madrugada, which means Ranch of the Valley of Dawn. One of my grandmothers was a poet. So while other people live on ranches named after saints or fleas or trees, we live where day begins.

Our days begin with chocolate to drink and bread to eat. Arcadia, our cook, puts pitchers and platters upon the dining room table. Tía breaks her fast while sitting down, like a lady. But the men remain standing, swallowing quickly so that they can get an early start on the day's task of supervising all the work that must be done on our ranch. Grego stands and gulps, too. I am not allowed to gulp. If I go into the dining room, Tía makes me sit down beside her.

So—if I think I can go without eating for a few hours—I pull on my pantaloons and sneak outside. I tell one of the servants to saddle another pony so that I can go out supervising, too.

The Wednesday after Easter I escaped into a morning that was fresh and cool. I shivered while I waited. Grego was the first to leave the dining room, and he was as righteous as God. "This is men's work," he told me.

But Papi only laughed.

I ignored Grego, kicked my pony and followed the *real* men: Grandfather and Papi, but not Uncle Isidro, who

18

was away on one of his trips. We ambled from the blacksmith to the saddlery. "Don Nico de Haro," the blacksmith said to my father. "Don Blas de Haro," the saddle maker said to my grandfather with an extra bow.

Grandfather nodded in return. But Papi only glanced at the work the men displayed; he only gave them the briefest instructions. Papi was too busy trying to reinterest Grandfather in an almost forgotten plan. "A gristmill!" Papi pronounced. "It's what we most need, Father!"

"Too American," Grandfather replied.

Grego and I kept our ponies in place while the adults talked. Grego tried to sit like a don, look like a don, so that anybody watching would think that he was participating in the conversation, too. But he was much too short.

I stopped listening. Instead I looked. To the eastern hills; to the western hills; to the north, where our valley widens all the way to the Sacramento River; to the south, where the valley narrows, on the way to the town of San José. It is all El Rancho de la Madrugada. We de Haros are the lords and ladies of a great, great land.

"You must recall, Father," Papi said. "I ordered the machinery—and millwrights, too—from the Boston merchants before the war. It may all be on its way to us now that the war has ended."

Boston! It's an almost impossible distance. But then, for us, everything is far: Our nearest neighbor is a half day's ride away. San José is even farther, and San

Francisco farther than that. Uncle Isidro's trips to and from Mexico City take two months of travel in each direction. But Boston! That's six months or more by sea. Boston is where most of the American merchant ships come from. We depend upon those ships for our luxuries. And necessities like pins and needles and chocolate. And maybe millwrights.

"Progress and improvement!" Papi boomed. "That is our future."

Grandfather harrumphed—a kind of refusal without words—which is what he usually does when Papi talks about progress. We continued onward, visiting the adobe maker, the carpenter, the irrigation pond. And then we returned home.

We walked together into the dining room for the second meal of the day—a real breakfast of meat and beans and chilies and coffee. "Oh, Cesa!" Tía scolded, for I stank of horses and happiness. "Go change!"

I was very hungry, so I dressed quickly and sped back. I found the little boys already gathered at our end of the table under the sad but watchful eye of Padre Tristan. Padre Tristan is a priest of the Cistercian order, our tutor, and purveyor of religion to everybody who lives on Rancho Madrugada. He doesn't smile and he never laughs. He isn't mean, just sad. In a holy way, I suppose. He was gone during most of Lent this year, borrowed by the mission in San Francisco. But he returned to us in time to cele-

20

brate Easter Mass in our western yard. We children call him Padre Mournful.

"Cesa!" Tía scolded again. For I still stood, wondering if Padre Mournful had smiled in San Francisco. And what that smile might have looked like. "*Assieds-toi,*" Tía ordered. Which means "sit down" in French. I sat, but in a Mexican way, not French. Like a horsewoman, not a lady. Tía was educated in a French convent—the best years of her life, as far as I can tell. She likes to speak French to me, and she always speaks French to Padre Mournful. He must teach English, mathematics and the best of Spanish literature—and speak French for his breakfast, dinner and supper. Perhaps that is why he never smiles.

I sat down and studied Padre Mournful's face for clues. Would we have school today or not? Often he cancels our lessons, being so busy with his religious duties.

"*Vraiment?*" Padre Mournful replied to Tía, telling me nothing.

Servants came in and out of the door to my right, bringing in food and taking out dishes. To my left there was another door that opened onto the veranda. Next to that door there was a window with small panes, its iron grille meant to discourage grizzly bears. A kitchen servant entered from the right, trailed by Majo, Tía's precious and horrible cat. *Tap, tap, tap:* On my left there was my favorite bird, Jayboy, feathers

21

blue and gray, hanging upside down from an iron bar and knocking at the window.

Majo wound his way among the ankles beneath the table. He paused to put a warning tooth against my leg before jumping onto Tía's lap. Tía petted with one hand and fed both herself and Majo with the other. A bite of tortilla for her; a morsel of shredded beef for Majo. *"Par conséquent...,"* she said to Padre Mournful. French, always French.

Majo jumped down from Tía's lap. He inspected around Cinco's chair, where there are often crumbs. Cinco, wary of Majo's teeth and claws, raised his legs straight out. But Cinco was watching. By now all of us children were watching: Majo approaching closer and closer to the veranda door, Jayboy swinging himself upside down, pecking the window with a taunting *tap, tap, tap.*

Greedy Majo, impudent Jayboy. And now Papi was watching, too. For one moment Majo was safe; in the next he crossed that invisible line that Jayboy considered to be the beginning of the outdoors, the beginning of bird territory. With a gleeful rush of wings Jayboy shot inside the doorway, just far enough within to peck the top of Majo's head. Majo jumped and screamed with fury; he clawed. But Jayboy had already retreated to the safe outdoors, laughing.

"That bird!" Tía was shocked back into Spanish.

"Is a Mexican bird," Papi approved.

"Does that mean Majo is American?" Cinco asked shyly.

"War!" Grego exclaimed.

"Mon Dieu!" Tía called upon God in French.

Padre Mournful looked sadly at Grego, then at Cinco. We children waited for a moral, perhaps a lecture on the evils of violence. But: "I have baptisms to perform and confessions to hear," Padre Mournful announced. "There will be no school today."

Hurray!

Tía rose. We children pushed back our chairs. Out in the corridor we hooted and laughed like a flock of jaybirds.

"Let's play war!" said Cuatro.

"No!" said Cinco, and he ran into the kitchen. The rest of us followed, curious.

The kitchen is Arcadia's domain. She has three helpers, but still she does most of the work. It's not that the girls are lazy, but that Arcadia is so busy. Up until a year ago, Arcadia was our nurse. But when Cinco turned five and no longer needed as much care, Arcadia put him under Padre Mournful's supervision. She took over the running of the kitchen.

"You may shell beans, you may chop chilies, you may grind corn," Arcadia snapped. She doesn't like to see idle hands.

Cinco obediently took a little bowl of beans and sat down upon the floor. Cuatro shook his head, but not so that Arcadia could see; Dos stepped very quietly. We edged toward the far door, the water barrel door. But then Tía sailed into the kitchen from the courtyard, carrying a bundle half as large as herself. "Outside!" she commanded the boys. "You stay, Cesa."

The boys escaped, but I couldn't. Tía looked me up and down. She shook her head. "Oh, Cesa." She despaired of me, always. I looked myself up and down. I had pulled a petticoat over my pantaloons for breakfast. My rough brown pantaloons drooped beneath the flounced yellow skirt hem. "When I tell you to change your clothes, I mean change!"

She became stern. "Take these linens to the washwomen," she instructed. "Observe. Make sure that the women are progressing well in their tasks, that they have enough soap. If they are not working as they should be, or if they do not have enough soap, come back and tell me. Now, go!"

I had to go. I had to accept Tía's bundle. I passed by my brothers, who were standing around the water barrel making noises like frogs. I passed the little water boy, who was lugging two buckets of water up the rise to our house. I followed the water boy's path down to the creek and then downstream, where the washwomen were sorting clothes and linens and colors and cloth. All of the washwomen were Indian servants, and they laughed and joked and chided, calling out to me in their separate languages—until I dropped my bundle and they saw that it was my face behind the linens. A lady of the land.

All of the chattering stopped. The head wash-woman stepped forward. *"Señorita,"* she said politely.

I didn't answer. I didn't observe and inspect and inquire about the soap like I was supposed to do. Instead I unfastened my petticoat, let it fall into the dirty clothes, and fled. Not back to my brothers and their silly games, but up into the hills, up to one of my most secret places. Because I was walking, my journey took hours. Two hours, maybe more. But I didn't mind. With Easter comes spring; after the winter's rains come flowers. I climbed bright green hillsides dotted with gold. I tucked sprigs of goldfields, wild mustard, and poppies into my braided hair. I was as wild and beautiful as any nymph. And then I saw Grandfather.

He was where I wanted to be, but he was on a horse. I sank into the grasses, hoping I would blend in, hoping he wouldn't see me. I didn't want to be sent home; I didn't want to intrude upon his solitude.

Grandfather was all alone, just as I sometimes like to be. He was all alone, and he was looking into my vernal pool.

It's mine because I found it a year or so after Mamá died. I found it on my own, and until now I thought it was a secret. I had ridden into the hills one day when I was too sad to cry, and I found a shallow dimple

25

of water that was hatching out salamanders and fairy shrimp. I came back often. And that's when I saw the miracle. Not a holy miracle with glowing saints and singing angels, but a miracle of nature. Day after day, as the pool evaporated into the dry spring air, new flowers grew around its shrinking edges. Rings of flowers, one kind within another: white meadowfoam surrounding purple downingia surrounding pink monkeyflower. Circles within circles of color. It was Mamá's gift to me, that's what I decided. I was only nine years old.

But the pool continued to shrink. It shrank until all the water was gone, evaporated away. The flowers died. It was as though Mamá had died again, too, and I cried.

But I came back. I came back again and again. Grasses covered the dimple—in midsummer I couldn't even find where it had been. I returned even through the winter rains. And then, one day, there was the pool! With new salamanders crawling from the water and new flowers growing! And I was happy.

I still return every spring to see the miracle, the blessing, that is my pool. But now Grandfather sat above my vernal pool, gazing and gazing at the white and the purple and the pink. His expression was so soft, so unkinglike, that I put my hands up to my own cheeks and chin. I wondered if my face looked like his face: a vision of hope.

Grandfather spurred his horse and turned toward

26

home. He still hadn't seen me. I waited until he was well away, and then I approached the pool. I had planned to dance around the pool like a pagan, with flowers tumbling from my hair. I had planned to sing a hymn to the Virgin Mary, that holiest of all mothers. But instead I put my feet where Grandfather's horse had left its hoofprints. The words that came from my throat were Tía's hymn of praise: "God's gift to mankind!" God's gift—not just to me, but to everybody. The gift of *la madrugada,* the dawn. The gift of Madrugada, the ranch.

Because I had to walk home, I missed dinner. I calculated my possible entries and decided upon secrecy. I circled the house, walking quietly into the western yard and then up onto the veranda where the servants were already taking their afternoon rest. I climbed through my open window and saw myself in my mirror. My clothes were disheveled, my hair still bright with meadow flowers. I stopped, reluctant to enter the dark. I balanced between inside and outside, shadow and sunlight. Then I decided: All things must come to an end. That is why we have rest and sleep and night—and dawn. So that we can reawaken to all the wonders yet to come.

Chapter 5

A Real American

The winds of May are always winds of change. Our constant breeze, usually from the west, shifts into a northern wind that blows for days. Beneath those dry, dry gusts the wild grasses turn from green to green-dusted bronze to gold. No longer soft, the grasslands are soon filled with tiny spurs that catch your legs. The world turns contrary, and so do our moods.

I was waiting, impatiently, for my brothers to prepare for battle. Grego was having his horse saddled: first a woven blanket over the horse's back, then the saddle tree, then the necessary leather housing, then an unnecessary leather covering stamped with silver and embroidered with colored threads.

I huffed. "You're going to look like a fiesta!"

Grego stood tall. Having grown two fingers higher

since Easter, he was now almost as tall as me. *"Yo soy El Uno! El Único!"* he told the world in a deep, deep voice. I am The One, The Only One.

"Bah!" I replied, just like Grandfather.

Dos began squabbling with Cuatro. "If I hit you with my rifle, that's enough!"

"It isn't!" Cuatro retorted.

"The killer must say *'zas.'*" Tres is always our judge in these matters. "A rifle kill doesn't count unless he says *'zas.'*"

And that is when the American rode up.

A real American! We hadn't seen one for almost two years, and this one was just as tall and bearded as I remembered them to be. He held his head as importantly as a magistrate or bishop—which he surely was not. He examined everything: the long, low, whitewashed adobe; the corral; the open shed where the saddles and bridles hung; the Indian servant mending a bench upon the veranda. The Indian put down his tools. My brothers and I stared. But the American only glanced at us and then rode past us as if we didn't matter. He stopped before the veranda and, still mounted, called out, *"Hola!"*

Papi stepped out from the parlor. *"Hola,"* he returned, surprised.

The American spoke again, in almost-good Spanish: "I'm Major John Allgood. Just passing through."

"Through to where?" Papi inquired.

"The Sierra Nevada."

Those are the great mountains far east of our ranch, maybe four days away by pony. Longer if you are herding sheep all the way across the great central valley and up to the summer pastures. Which is what our shepherds do every May.

"There're stories of gold up there," the American continued. "How much gold, I don't know. But I'm going to find out."

"Gold!" Grego exclaimed; his voice was very loud. But the American didn't look back at us.

"I've heard rumors." Papi was perfectly polite. "I am Don Nicolás de Haro, and I welcome you to El Rancho del Valle de la Madrugada."

I nodded with Papi in welcome. Before the war Rancho Madrugada welcomed all visitors, of all nationalities. Including Americans. Now that the war was over, our customs continued unchanged.

I waited for Papi to extend his courtesies: to invite the American to dismount, to call for a servant to care for the American's horse, to call for Tía to prepare a bed so that the American could spend the night and rest up for the remainder of his journey. But Papi didn't. Instead he said, "Will you remain here for a moment?" and stepped back inside.

"Something's wrong," I told Grego.

Grego wouldn't listen. "Gold!" he said to Dos.

I went inside, too—around the American and his horse, up onto the veranda, into the parlor. And there was Grandfather sitting stiffly in the great chair that is his and only his. Grandfather's head was turned from the windows; his face was as stern and unchangeable as truth.

"Father." Papi spoke quietly because the American wasn't all that far away.

"I will offer no hospitality." Grandfather's word was final. "I welcome no Americans."

Papi closed his eyes, a silent kind of sigh.

But we must! I wanted to shout. I couldn't, though, not at Grandfather. Hospitality to all, questions to none—that's the California way. It's a tradition that every family follows, a tradition that's almost holy. A tradition that had never been broken before, not at Rancho Madrugada, not in my lifetime.

I felt something bump against my hip: Cinco. "Maybe Grandfather is sad because of the winds," Cinco whispered.

Grandfather would not relent. Papi had to return to the veranda with only kind words to offer: "If you go around the house, sir, our cook will give you food. I wish you well on your journey."

Cinco left the veranda to rejoin our brothers, but I reentered the house. I walked through the parlor, where Grandfather and Papi were arguing. They often disagree, but this argument was harsh. Papi almost raised his voice. "The war is over, Father."

Grandfather was not so restrained. "I will admit no American to be our equal!"

Sounds of their discord followed me into the courtyard.

31

I closed the door to the kitchen, shutting it out. I passed along Papi's wishes, even though he hadn't yet asked me to do so. "We are to give food to a traveling American," I told Arcadia.

"An American!" Arcadia immediately began ordering her maids. One tied cold tamales into a napkin; another sliced beef. Arcadia herself poured wine into a flask. When the American arrived at the back door he let his horse drop its head into the water barrel that is reserved for our cooking and drinking. Which was rude. Arcadia handed up the food and wine; she and I, together, watched the American ride away.

Grandfather's voice, so loud, so angry, suddenly penetrated the kitchen door, rose over the kitchen clatter. Arcadia frowned.

"It's the winds," I told her. "It's only the May winds. Here, I'll help." I took the hollow gourd that hung from the water barrel and I began to scoop. I scooped out all the scum of horse slobber; I scooped out the floating dust and bugs and twigs—all the debris of May. I scooped out Grandfather's great anger and my own bad humor. I scooped out everybody's disagreeableness. And when Grego finally found me, riding his horse and leading mine, my mind was made up.

"Are you ready?" he asked.

"The war is over," I informed him. "Even in games."

"Well?" Grego was impatient. "What do you want to do, then?"

We ended up tracking the American as he passed

through our land. We stalked from a distance, the five boys and me. The American again acted as if he didn't know we were there. The little boys mocked his seat.

"Look!" said Dos, and he let his hips roll in an exaggerated way, his bottom bounce.

"He rides like Arcadia!" Cuatro jeered.

Jesús was up ahead, on his pony, observing a small herd of cattle. Jesús is a very important person on our ranch. Like us de Haros, he is a Californio, a descendent of Spain born in California. Once he was our head vaquero; he supervised the 150 horsemen that tend our cattle. Now he's too old. But still, in his own way, Jesús is a king, something like Grandfather. His expression when the American shouted, *"Hola!"* was one of polite disdain. My brothers and I rode right up to listen.

"Some say there's a fortune in gold in those mountains," the American told Jesús. "I figure that one of those fortunes just might be mine."

"Gold!" Our newest vaquero, who was accompanying Jesús, licked his lips as if gold were something that he could taste.

But, "Our gold," Jesús instructed, almost in Grandfather's tones, "is our land. The de Haro land." He waved his arm as if to encompass the world.

"Well," the American said, "I suppose it's American land now."

I couldn't help myself. I burst out, "No! That's not true!"

Jesús looked at me hard, as if to tell me, *We are Californios; we are too lofty to argue with a mere American.* Jesús spurred his pony away from the American, a snub the American had certainly earned.

The American didn't even know what a snub was. "I'll ride with you some," he invited himself.

Jesús simply continued with his plans for the day.

Jesús and the American—and my brothers and I— all rode to the edge of a canyon not far from Madrugada Creek. During the rainy season the canyon is high with rushing water, but in the winds of May it is dry. Down in the canyon, Gaspár, Jesús's son—and now our head vaquero—was training a pony. Eight mounted vaqueros watched and made comments.

"Cho! Cesa!" Gaspár wasn't saying my name. Instead, he was teaching the pony to come to a sudden stop from a full gallop—as every good cow pony must do the moment a steer is lassoed.

My brothers began to drift down the canyon wall. Each of my brothers has his favorite vaquero; the boys try to look, ride and speak as much like their heroes as possible. Cuatro's face became suddenly solemn; he halted next to a Californio with exactly that expression. Dos's favorite Indian rode bareback; Dos dismounted to loosen his cinch.

"Fíjate!" the Indian said to Dos. Watch me. And then he began to show off. Not to Dos, but to the American, I think. Because it's a truth that everybody

knows: Americans cannot handle ropes. The other vaqueros began to toss their lariats, too: overhand, underhand, from over their heads. Eight lariats whizzing through the air like eight hissing snakes, sometimes nicking each other but never tangling.

"*Hombres!*" Gaspár called out. And his vaqueros pulled in their lariats. Gaspár looked up the canyon wall, directly at the American. Gaspár bowed from his saddle. "*Americano!*" Gaspár's word was a challenge.

He took a gold American ten-dollar piece from his pocket, made sure that everybody saw what it was, and then threw it down the length of the canyon, toward the creek. Everybody watched to see exactly where the coin would disappear into the yellowed grasses. As soon as gold blended into gold, Gaspár spurred his pony to a full gallop. They rushed down the canyon, the half-trained pony smashing and pounding grasses into the soil. Gaspár, heedless of danger, slipped sideways in his saddle until his head dropped lower than the pony's knees. He reached into the grasses, his hand a flicker of movement between the flashing hooves. He pulled himself up into his saddle again. He slid the pony to an almost proper stop.

"Observe!" Gaspár shouted. He held up his right hand: A tiny circle above his fingers glinted bright yellow.

"Yip! Yip! Yip!" cried the vaqueros.

Jesús and I applauded. The American raised his hands, admitting defeat before even trying to compete, admitting another truth that everybody knows:

Americans cannot handle horses. But all he said was, "So there's gold in your land after all."

I went down into the canyon, to where Grego was as gleeful as any vaquero. "However did the Americans win the war?" Grego shouted. "They are nothing, nothing to us!" My other brothers laughed. Then: "Cesa," Grego said, "I challenge you to a coin race!"

For a moment I hesitated. But then I remembered something Mamá used to say: *It isn't only gold that glitters, it isn't only roosters that crow.*

"Agreed!" I almost felt that I was following Mamá's advice: Let the American see what a Californio *woman* could do! "Tres, set the course!"

"To the oak tree," Tres decided. "Up the canyon wall. Around that clump of chaparral. Down to the gulch, jumping across. Up the far side to the buckeye tree, jump again. Race to the finish line, here." He drew a line with his hand in the air, indicating where we stood.

"Agreed?" Grego said to me.

"Yes!"

It took some searching of pockets, but we collected four small coins. Grego and I held our knees tight against our saddles; carefully we tucked a coin between each knee and saddle. Our goal was to ride Tres's course, come in first, and never drop a coin.

"Put your ponies side by side," Tres told us. "Prepare."

We prepared.

"Santiago!" Tres shouted.

We galloped, our bodies as close to our ponies' necks as possible, our knees clutching the ponies' sides like the jaws of a vise. We were head to head until we reached the last, drooping branch of the oak. I turned my pony first, before Grego. My knees rubbed against my saddle as my pony pushed me up the canyon wall. With each bump I held my knees in closer; an ache grew in my hips, in my back. I circled the clump of chaparral before Grego, but I could hear his pony breathing at my back. Down the canyon wall, and I let my pony slide a bit—not to a stop, but to increase its speed downhill. Over to the gulch, where I let the pony judge the jump. I concentrated on my knees; the coins still held. Up the far side of the gulch to the buckeye tree, a tree that my brothers and I have known since we were infants. It is a lower, smaller tree than the oak.

And now, in this month of May, the buckeye had leaves like bright green fingers. Its branches held up long, white flowers. Green fingers, white fingers. And dancing over them all, a host of butterflies. We call the butterflies goldenspots. Some have black wings, some have red wings, but they are all marked with little yellow spots. I had never seen so many gathered at once; there must have been hundreds. Green and white, black and red. Flashes of gold. That tree was an amazement of color.

And I, in my amazement, lifted my back and loosened

my knees. I stayed stopped in time—while my pony rushed forward.

My brothers and I had all learned how to fall as well as how to ride, back in those days when we could barely talk. So even when we forget ourselves completely—as I did before the buckeye tree—our bodies know how to roll and protect themselves. My body did its best. While my eyes still saw golden flashes and green growth, my knees and arms and head tucked. But my right foot, instead of toeing the stirrup, had somehow become settled all the way in. And so my ankle turned as I tucked, and I felt the pain all the way into my teeth.

"Cesa!" Grego was first to my side. His coins, mine—we never saw them again.

"Cesa!" My little brothers were soon overtaken by the men, who could ride harder, faster.

I gritted my teeth and tried not to cry.

"Cesa . . ." Jesús was exasperated but gentle.

One of the Indians left his pony to bring me the stem of a poppy flower. "Put this in your mouth," he directed. "Chew."

I chewed. I didn't cry.

"Oh, Cesa." And now Jesús was sitting on the ground beside me, his hands testing my leg, my ankle. "A sprain, I think, not a break." He took the sash from his waist and began to bind my ankle tightly. "So many ways to occupy yourself—and you do this. Even your good mother never rode so crazily. Such a fine woman—and yet sometimes I think she was greatly at fault in failing to give you a sister as a companion."

I couldn't respond. But I did glance up the canyon. The American was gone, off to find his gold. We could continue with our lives unchanged. Again. Good!

Chapter 6

Hortencia Goes Hunting

Maybe I never had a sister, but I do have dozens of cousins. Jesús told Tía that I needed a female companion; Tía looked at my ankle and spoke to Papi; Papi agreed. Uncle Isidro was given the task. This time, when he returned home from San Francisco, he brought with him a cousin five years older than me.

Hortencia: all ribbons and feathers and sidesaddle. Everything that she wore was blue, even her boots. She sat upon her horse—a very nice light-colored mustang with silver mane and tail—and tinkled her laughter down upon us all. "So big!" she cooed when she saw me and my brothers. "So tall!" She held her hands out, like flat little offerings, so that Uncle Isidro would help her down from her sidesaddle. She stayed close to him for just an instant, and then she turned to Tía.

"Cousin Graciela! It's been so long!" She kissed Tía's cheek, her big blue hat with its even bluer feathers knocking Tía's hair comb askew. Then she grabbed me. "We're to be sister-cousins, Cesa!"

"Uh," I grunted, for Hortencia squeezed hard.

Uncle Isidro glanced down at my still-bandaged ankle. "Cesa." He patted my head, then turned to fol low Papi and Grandfather into the house.

"Oh, Isidro!" Hortencia trilled, but Uncle Isidro didn't look back.

Hortencia sighed, an exaggerated gesture. "He must be talking about the Americans," she confided to Tía. "There're so many Boston ships now at the port. So many Americans, and all of them talking about gold. Have you seen any Americans out here?"

"Only one recently," Tía answered. "Major John Allgood."

"Why, I know him!" Hortencia clapped her hands with delight. "Don't you think he's handsome?"

"Please," Tía said to our guest, and I thought she sounded just a little bit resigned, "come inside."

We went inside. Hortencia walked slowly through the parlor. Like the American's, her eyes examined everything: Grandfather's great carved chair, the bureau on which we keep a silver tray filled with coins for whoever might need them, the tattered sofa that five boys had almost kicked to shreds. Hortencia clicked her tongue when she saw that. Then into the dining room, where for the first time I realized that our massive table

41

is both old and scratched. Into the corridor, where Hortencia glanced in every doorway we passed, sometimes shaking her head, sometimes frowning. Servants followed us, laden with boxes and bags and a trunk.

When Hortencia entered my room—she and I would have to share—she stopped just inside the doorway, leaving the servants to pile up behind her like debris behind an irrigation clog. "Ah," she said, finally pleased with something, "a canopy."

I have a canopy bed, and so does Grandfather. At first I didn't understand what a canopy bed meant to Hortencia, because for those first few days her words were always complimentary. I trailed her about the house—there wasn't much else I could do because of my ankle—and watched her. Hortencia would pick up a vase, handle it, turn it around, and say, "Spanish. Very pretty." Or a bowl and say, "From India, I think. Excellent brass." But then her tone began to change. She didn't exactly criticize our furniture; instead she described, in detail, the furnishings at her father's rancho and those of other ranchos near San Francisco, where every bedroom, it seemed, had a new canopy bed made of South American mahogany. "It could all be done here, too, Cesa," she told me. "With all of your land and cattle. With all the hides and tallow you have to trade. With all of your wealth. Rancho Madrugada could become a showplace."

"What for?" I replied.

"Oh, Cesa!" Hortencia tinkled her laugh at me. She took me by the hand and led me, like an infant, to Tía.

Tía was sitting on a bench in the courtyard, surrounded by her plants and flowers. I sometimes look at Tía's courtyard garden and wonder if maybe I don't really know Tía very well. She never wears colors, only an old woman's, a widow's, black. But she grows camellias, roses, nasturtiums, and marigolds. She chooses flowers for their color, shape and size, and grows them in pots according to the season. She is very particular about the pots—our Indians make them and glaze them with red and yellow and orange designs. There's only one spot of black in the garden—Tía's gown. Somehow, around that black, all the colors glow brighter.

Now Tía sat with Majo purring on her lap. One of her hands stroked Majo, the other lay still. It isn't often that Tía's hands are silent. It isn't often that she sits with a dreamy expression on her face. It isn't often that she rests.

"Just think!" Hortencia said, and Tía blinked. "Little Cesa sees no need for change! She believes that Rancho Madrugada is perfect! Complete!"

Little Cesa was pulled over to a bench and made to sit next to Hortencia, who continued to pat Little Cesa's hand as though it were a tortilla in the making.

"But oh, just think what could happen if the right person were set to the task! The Boston ships at San

43

Francisco have the most wonderful things to trade: painted furniture from New England, rosewood furniture from the Orient, the most beautiful carpets. Brocaded sofas. Canopy beds."

"Well—" Tía began.

But Hortencia interrupted Tía. "I know that your chores are many, Cousin Graciela. Too many, actually. You have little time to consider such matters. But with a little help . . ." And Hortencia turned to me, my hand now as limp and flat as it could ever be. "Wouldn't you like to have a little aunt, Cesa? A sweet little aunt, to make life ever so much more comfortable?"

"So that's why she *really* came," I later told Grego. "Not to be my sister-cousin, but to become our 'little aunt'!"

"Well, Uncle Isidro isn't interested," Grego replied.

Which was true. Later that day, when we were all out in the western yard, Jayboy dived from the air to attack Hortencia's hat. Hortencia screeched. Dramatically, she leaned toward Uncle Isidro for protection; she pretended to swoon.

But Uncle Isidro didn't even notice. He was laughing with us, for Jayboy flew off with a feather even bluer than himself. "That bird is as territorial as an old Californio," Uncle Isidro guffawed. He was obviously less interested in Hortencia than in her hat.

Things didn't look promising for Hortencia. But love, it seems, is another kind of war. Hortencia

44

changed tactics. For the first time in her visit she opened her trunk. I sat on my bed and watched while she lifted out gown after gown of the most gorgeous silk. They were formal clothes, fancy clothes, with low necklines and full skirts—as beautiful as anything I had ever imagined. I slid down from my bed to help. I held each gown up before my mirror and wondered: How would I look in ice blue brocade? Or in teal green embroidered with tiny houses? I would be a true *princesa* dressed in such silk!

"The fabric is from China." Hortencia was crisp with important decisions to make; she wasn't enthralled by beauty. "Bought, of course, from a Boston trader's ship. And most of the patterns are American—Americans have such fashion! Look at these, Cesa." She spread a pair of gilt-lace-edged pantalets out on my bed. "Now, these are guaranteed to make a gentleman *think*."

Just as there are rules in war, there are rules for catching a man. That night, as we lay together beneath my canopy, Hortencia talked. "First, be as proper and modest as possible. That satisfies both your mother and his. Second—and this is far more important—wear your prettiest clothes."

She talked on, but I fell asleep. Like Uncle Isidro, I wasn't interested. But the next night I listened, because Hortencia told of balls she had attended that lasted all night long. Of picnics where ten or more families gathered to laugh and eat from noon until midnight. Of wedding fiestas where the music continued for a full week, people dozing in their chairs and then awakening to dance again.

While Hortencia told her stories, I began to remember my own. When Mamá was alive we hosted parties. Family and friends came from as far away as Monterey to celebrate my brothers' births. How could I have forgotten that? Everybody feasted, laughed and danced. Even us children. And always, the center of greatest happiness was Mamá. She was so very beautiful.

"Mamá once wore a gown with lavender lace," I interrupted Hortencia. "She wore lilacs in her hair."

"And a corsage of violets," Hortencia added. "It was when Cuatro was born."

"You remember, too?" I rolled over to face Hortencia, pushing myself up onto an elbow. "What did Mamá say? What did she do? Tell me more!"

But Hortencia had her own thoughts to finish. "These are the things that make a girl happy," she instructed. "Parties and gowns and a home furnished American style, from a Boston trader's ship."

"But Mamá!" I begged.

Hortencia wasn't listening to me; Mamá wasn't important to her. "Rancho Madrugada has such potential. It could give me everything I want."

I stared. Was that the *real* reason why Hortencia had come to us? Not because she truly loved Uncle

Isidro, but because she wanted what Mamá had: our land, our wealth? Our ranch?

There she lay, a greedy lump on one of *my* pillows. I slid out of bed, ripped off a blanket, and lay by myself on the floor.

"Cesa?" Hortencia was too sleepy to really care.

I clutched the blanket around me and waited. I waited for morning and a chance to talk with Grego. But somehow I slept through Tía's song. I didn't catch Grego until after second breakfast.

"Grego!" I grabbed his arm to make him pay attention. "What Hortencia really wants is to be mistress of Rancho Madrugada. She wants our ranch."

We stood in the corridor, looking into the parlor. Hortencia sat on the tattered sofa with her ankles crossed and her gilt-lace-edged pantalets just showing between hem and shoe. With her silver thimble she daintily sewed buttons onto a shirt for Uncle Isidro. Uncle Isidro sat opposite her, on a cowhide chair, reading.

"Oh, Isidro." Hortencia held up the shirt, but to the side, so as to not cover her gown.

Uncle Isidro glanced at the shirt, then at her pantalets. He smiled.

"Mother of God!" I groaned.

Grego raised his eyebrows at me as if to ask, *Do you think it could really happen?*

"Yes!" I hissed.

I wanted to talk more, but Grego was on his way outdoors, where our little brothers were waiting. "Grego! Cesa!" They were out by the corral, shouting, yipping, calling to us. "Hurry!"

I had to hold all my words inside. It was a *matanza* day, the day when we harvested our ranch's wealth, and the boys were so excited.

"Cesa!" Cuatro was impatient.

I began to mount a pony on my own but needed help because of my ankle. Strong Dos had to boost me up. "Race you!" Tres said. And we all raced. I raced until my heart pounded and I could feel my pulse pound, too. Even my ankle throbbed—with pain.

Still, we were almost late. When we reached the *matanza* field the vaqueros were already there, 150 strong men on swift horses circling a herd of maybe a thousand cattle.

"Ah!" said Dos, and we held our ponies back to watch.

Gaspár raised his hand; he let it fall. At the signal a dozen vaqueros left the circle and moved into the herd. They rode as if their ponies were part of their legs, walking slowly, constantly. They leaned left and right, flashing knives in their hands. Behind them cattle fell, almost instantly killed. A knife into a neck here; a knife into a neck there. And then the living cattle, at first slow to react, began to shift and turn.

"It's beginning," Dos said. And now he, I and all of

my brothers were almost breathless, although it was not we who moved so dangerously in the midst of the restless herd. "There!"

It was as though the cattle awakened: first asleep in their understanding, then suddenly knowing dread. They panicked; they rushed; they charged the riders. The ponies responded with speed and skill. Animals tried to escape; the circling vaqueros drove them back. Back into the herd. Back into death. Back into a field of golden grasses now dripping with red. One thousand cattle. It was a very large kill.

And it was all over soon, really. My brothers and I left when the strippers arrived, those Indians who cut the hides from the bodies. And the women who cut and render the tallow. We left before their knives made the field slick with blood.

"One thousand hides," Grego calculated. "And enough tallow, I'm sure, to pay the Boston trader for the millstones that Papi ordered. That, and passage for the millwrights. Papi's had a message, Cesa—they're coming now that the war is over. The money's already committed. Grandfather has to agree. We'll soon have a mill to grind corn and wheat." Grego was already thinking practical thoughts, money matters, ways of turning the wealth of the *matanza* back into our ranch.

But my blood still boiled. My blood. Cattle blood. Blood spilling into the soil of Rancho Madrugada.

There is no wealth that is separate from who and what we are. We are as much part of the land as the mosquitoes, flies and wasps that were now celebrating a meal they could drown in. As the foxes, bobcats and grizzlies that would soon gather to eat from carcasses left upon the field. People, cattle, insects, bears: We are all Rancho Madrugada.

Mamá was Rancho Madrugada. Hortencia was most definitely not. "Grego." I made him slow down to listen to me. "Hortencia has to leave."

I didn't have to think very hard; I knew what to do. As always after a *matanza,* the men left the house in the early evening. They went to hunt the animals that were still gorging on the killing field. Hortencia sat alone on the veranda. Grego and I came to sit beside her, one on each side. We looked over at the corral, emptied of all the best ponies. Only the best-trained horse can withstand the sight and sound and smell of a grizzly bear. Hortencia's silver-maned mustang had been left behind.

"Oh, dear," I sighed.

"What's wrong, Cesa?" Grego followed my script exactly.

"I wish we were hunting, too."

"Not until we're older." And then Grego added, as though it were an afterthought, "There's nothing Uncle Isidro enjoys more than seeing a woman out hunting."

That's all it took. That, and some help: While Grego

saddled Hortencia's horse, I buttoned her into her blue riding habit. She insisted upon wearing her hat with the feathers, as she wanted to look her best. By the time we finished, bats were flying in the air. Grego gave Hortencia's horse a solid slap on its rump. "That way," he said, and pointed.

I limped into my room and lay down beneath my canopy, luxuriously alone. I intended to lie awake, to wait. But I fell asleep to the hoot of a great horned owl—and was roused almost immediately by loud, gulping sobs: Hortencia, supported by Tía and a housemaid while two other housemaids followed with candles and a washing tub. Hortencia's hat was gone; her hair fell down around her shoulders. The back of her skirt was almost black. When a maid unbuttoned the blue habit, I could see that Hortencia's rump was greatly bruised. "Oh!" she moaned. She was covered with blood, but none of it was her own: It was all cattle blood. It washed off.

I sat up in bed, but Tía wouldn't look at me. Instead she very tenderly rubbed balm onto Hortencia's rump and then prepared her for bed. She covered Hortencia with my coverlet and briefly, gently, kissed her forehead.

"Tía?" I said.

Tía only sniffed angrily before she left my room.

I lay back down, as far away as I could get from Hortencia. Her sobs were less gulping now; sometimes she shuddered. "I didn't know that there would be *bears* out there!" she said. "I didn't know that I would be in the way! Isidro called me a fool!" Hortencia cried until she was almost asleep. "I have to leave," she said, "immediately. I can't stay here. Not where I am unwelcome and scorned."

Hortencia finally slept, but I didn't. It wasn't Tía's sniff that kept me awake, but a sort of weight that was seeping into my soul. I still felt right about some things: Hortencia had to leave, for she could never become mistress of Rancho Madrugada. But perhaps she could have gone another way. Maybe I hadn't needed to be quite so cruel.

With some remorse, I put my hand into sleeping Hortencia's hand—a belated gesture of comfort. "There, there," I said. "There, there."

Chapter 7

Penance

Padre Mournful always speaks to us in English because Papi asked him to, all those years ago when Padre Mournful first came to us from his monastery up in Canada. Papi thinks it important that we learn the language that belongs to the other half of the continent. Papi is very progressive.

So it was in English that Padre Mournful heard my confession after Hortencia left Rancho Madrugada. In English, and with a lot of sighs on his part. "Cesa," he said, "why? What compelled you to harm the spirit—not to mention the body—of a guest of this house?"

"She wanted to invade our house with furniture," I muttered.

"Invade the house?" Padre Mournful repeated. "Cesa, you make no sense at all."

53

"*American* furniture," I explained.

Padre Mournful became stern. "You have committed a sin against charity," he said. "I want you to reflect upon this lesson: Charity is more than hospitality, it is compassion." He reverted to the usual Latin prayers, ending my confession. He turned aside the confessional screen so that he could shake his head at me, sadly.

I waited outside until Grego had made his confession, too. "Seven rosaries a day for the next seven days," Grego reported. "All on my knees."

"The same penance for me," I told him. "And a lesson on charity."

A lesson, a scolding: They sound about the same in any language. We weren't finished yet. Next it was Tía's turn. She chose Spanish.

"A guest in our home!" Unlike Padre Mournful, Tía wasn't sad, she was angry. Perhaps it's easier to be angry in Spanish. "You two have insulted a long tradition of hospitality—a hospitality for which Rancho Madrugada was once famous! It doesn't matter that Hortencia is perhaps a bit silly—it isn't as though you two haven't been silly in your time. A Californio woman, Cesa, is a person of kindness! And Grego, how many times must I tell you: Just because Cesa has an idea, it doesn't mean it's a good one!"

"Hortencia was a *threat*," I said ominously.

"To what?" Tía snapped back. "Cesa, you are not only unkind, you are absurd. You and Grego will spend the next seven days in your rooms with no company or conversation."

54

I entered my room like a prisoner of war, obedient on the outside but everything inside churning in protest. I carried a rosary and an expanse of white linen, for embroidery was to be part of my sentence. I crawled into my window alcove so that I could look out upon freedom. But not one of the servants on the veranda spoke to me or even smiled. Tía's word ruled the world.

I sat down with my back against one side of the alcove, my feet pushing against the other side. I stabbed a needle into the linen. Stab! Hortencia was a threat. Stab! How could Tía not have seen that?

I yelped when I stabbed my finger, printing a spot of blood on the linen. Did I care? No. Did it matter? Maybe. I decided to embroider the spot of red into a rose. A red rose on a trailing grapevine. Tía probably wouldn't even notice.

I was making the rose especially big, especially red, when a rock hit my shoulder—as if I were indeed a great sinner. I was being stoned! Furious, I snatched up the rock, ready to hurl it back at whoever had condemned me. But it was a piece of paper tied around a rock with string. And outside in the yard—walking about, kicking up dust, doing nothing—was Dos. It was a message from Grego!

Dear Cesa,

Tía can't keep the little boys from talking all of the time, so this is what's happening. Our newest vaquero has left the ranch to hunt for gold in the mountains. Write back.

55

I couldn't write back: I had no paper, no ink. I shrugged at Dos pantomiming that I had nothing to write with.

Dos understood. He flashed a grin at me and ambled away. I settled back into my sewing, but this time I had something to think about: the mountains. The high Sierra Nevada meadows are luscious and green when ours are brittle and dry. We take our sheep up there to spend the summer. The rams, the ewes, the lambs. Even the little bummers, the orphans.

It was Mamá who insisted that the orphans be saved, fed by hand, cared for. That was so long ago. I even heard Mamá sing to them once. So that they wouldn't feel forsaken.

I was forsaken.

By the time Jesús knocked on my door, some hours later, I had gone from anger to sadness.

"Hello," I said with a hurting loneliness.

Jesús didn't answer. He put down my dinner tray and held up a long strip of winding cloth. I knew what it was for: My ankle had somehow gotten worse the day of the *matanza*. I held my foot out to him. Jesús can work wonders. Two years ago he cured Uncle Isidro's favorite saddle horse, which some of the vaqueros had claimed would never be able to run again.

"Did Gaspár finally free the bull that was stuck in the arroyo?" I asked. "Did the bay mare deliver her foal?"

Jesús only shook his head, still refusing to talk to

56

me. But I could almost hear his thoughts: *Oh, Cesa.* He left.

I returned to my window. Now I was sad and frustrated. And angry again, too. I picked up my needle and stabbed. I stabbed recklessly. I accidentally sewed the linen onto the knee of my pantaloons. What should I do? I could undo everything—too much work—or I could just snip off part of my pantaloons, leaving a hole for somebody else to mend.

I snipped. Then I snipped some more. I would appliqué a brown winter gourd onto the grapevine. See if Tía noticed that!

I appliquéd the gourd, then embroidered a chili pepper. A rock hit my leg.

Grandfather says that Papi can go ahead with the mill.

My door opened—this time without a knock. Tía came through like an avenging angel. She marched right up to my alcove and held out her hand.

I had to relinquish the note.

Oh, Cesa! Again, I only heard her thoughts—silent, but very, very clear. Tía shut the door behind her, loudly, so that I would understand: Grego and I could expect to be punished for the rest of our lives.

I looked out my window. This time I felt despair.

Maybe because I wanted to hear—somebody, anybody—I opened my ears. I listened. The sounds that came to me were not human, but they soothed. My day, Rancho Madrugada's day, passed with the click of the hummingbird, the mew of the hawk, the coo of the dove. I looked beyond veranda and yard to the hills dotted with oak, darkened with bay and buckeye, made sweet with gooseberry and wild rose. And haloed by the setting sun.

"Good night," I whispered. Not to a person, but to the ranch. I didn't feel so alone, not any longer. Once in a while I have to remind myself: I may not have a mother to love, but I have a ranch. It's not quite, but it's almost, the same.

Chapter 8

Californio Women

"I see a hummingbird chasing a wren, a goldfinch chasing a flicker, a kestrel chasing an owl." Arcadia stood outside the kitchen doorway—not the door that faces the courtyard, but the one that opens onto the wide and wonderful world. "When the small birds chase the larger ones, the gods are troubled. The birds are an omen of conflict."

"Nonsense!" Tía rejected Arcadia's thoughts with one word.

My week of solitude over, I had been released. But I was still a prisoner. Grego had to spend an extra two days in his room. I, who had only innocently received his messages, had to cook.

Tía was making me grind corn. I knelt on the dirt floor—just like one of Arcadia's maids—and turned the heavy stone against the granite bowl of the metate. The grinding stone was just big enough for one hand, and sometimes I had to switch. The hard, dry kernels slowly powdered. My left hand wasn't as strong as my right. My hands ached, my back ached, my knees ached. For the first time I fully realized, deep inside my bones, why Rancho Madrugada needed a mill. "Once it's built," I told the kitchen, "these metates will become doorstops!"

Arcadia slapped the cornmeal into tortillas, which we ate for dinner. There were only four of us at the table that day: Grandfather, Tía, Padre Mournful, and me. Grego ate from a tray in his room. Uncle Isidro was in San Francisco again. Papi and my younger brothers had gone off to wander the ranch and look for possible mill sites—to ride through the hills, to eat outside, to enjoy life.

"It's a grapevine." Tía spoke in French. She was describing my white linen, which now was almost an altar cloth. Padre Mournful, with polite interest, urged her to continue. "The vine has fruit—and flowers, and even some vegetables of autumn." Tía stopped, perplexed. "It's unusual. Perhaps creative. Certainly unique."

Well!

Grandfather, at the head of the table, ignored all the *"Mais oui!"*s coming from our end of the table. Grandfather is the perfect picture of a Californio man. He always dresses formally, in an embroidered waistcoat and short velvet jacket and nasturtium-white shirt—

even when he rides way back into the hills to inspect cattle. His face is serious, his back straight and proud. He smiles as rarely as Padre Mournful, not because he is sad but because he has so many important things to think about. Ranch things.

Tap, tap, tap! My ears instantly cheered up. Jayboy hung from the window grille, swinging and tapping. Majo was perched on Tía's lap. Jayboy screeched a challenge. Majo jumped down and went to stand at the invisible line that marked the cat/bird border. He growled a response.

I held my breath. Majo, deliberately, put one paw over the line. And then Jayboy was in the doorway. Teeth and claws, wings and beak: a clash of fur and feathers. Both Grandfather and I leaned from our chairs.

"Ay!" Tía called out.

Padre Mournful rose, as if to intervene, but cat and bird separated on their own, still screeching, still hissing. Jayboy left some feathers on Majo's territory, but he flew off with a solid clump of fur. Majo, spitting, jumped for the safe haven of Tía's lap.

"It's a deadlock," I judged.

Padre Mournful sighed. But Grandfather's eyes laughed, just a little—although his face was as stern as ever. And then, with the slightest upturning of his lips, Grandfather smiled, just for me. Just to agree. To share. I smiled back, surprised. My brothers think that Grandfather is strict, but maybe he isn't. Not completely.

61

Dinner, then siesta. After siesta, we women cooked again. Before dinner we had cooked in Spanish. This time we cooked in French. *"Alors!"* Tía said, and I sighed, as deeply as Padre Mournful ever did. "We will make a pastry, such as I learned to make when I was a pupil at the convent of Saint Genevieve in Mexico City," Tía declared.

Only I understood the French. Arcadia, excluded by language, told her kitchen maids to be ready for orders and announced that she and her girls were prepared to serve Doña Graciela.

"Pears," Tía said to me and only to me. "Butter."

I translated. Arcadia sent one of the kitchen maids to the orchard to pick the ripest of the summer pears. "Butter," she muttered, for that's an ingredient we rarely have in our kitchen. "Concia!" And it was that maid's job to make butter. "There were no cows in this country before the Spaniards came," Arcadia announced. "None were needed." Which was Arcadia's way of telling us all that she was offended.

Tía was too lofty to notice—or care. "Sugar," she said. Which is *sucre* in French and *azúcar* in Spanish.

This time Arcadia understood without translation. She ordered the third kitchen maid to grind a hard lump of sugar down to grains on a clean metate. "Hmpf!" said Arcadia.

Tía put her finger to the metate. She tasted the sugar. She smiled at me. "At the convent we also cooked with sugar from Peru," she reminisced. And

62

her face was somehow softer in French, made almost pretty by memories of her girlhood. "Peru . . . and I had thought that Mexico City was the end of the world. I lost my mother when I was young, as you did, Cesa. But I was sent away to school. At first I cried. But then I came to love the convent. We learned to draw, to dance, to sing—the French nuns are a merry sort! I thought that I would live there forever, maybe become a Californio-French nun myself." Tía paused, caught in the past.

Arcadia took advantage of Tía's silence. "My great-great-grandmother saw the first cow, brought by Spanish warriors traveling with Spanish priests." This time Arcadia spoke in her own language, that of the Tatcan people, which Tía does not understand but I do. "The priests bought the souls of my great-great-grandmother's village, and the warriors bought the land, all for the price of a few silver spoons," Arcadia told me.

Tía heard, but she didn't. To her, Arcadia's Tatcan voice was only chatter, a rise and fall of Indian breath. Tía took Concia's butter and kneaded it with flour, salt and sugar. She patted the dough inside a piece of heavy pottery. She reached into the basket of pears that Arcadia held. She sliced the pears very thin.

"I learned to make this pastry with apples." Tía's voice was so gentle I had to lean close to hear. "But pears do very well. The French can cook with anything. I ate French, I dreamt in French, I almost was

63

French. And then my father, your great-grandfather, came all the way to Mexico City to tell me that I was to be married. Which I was. And widowed soon thereafter." Tía's sigh was one of enormous loss.

"The Spaniards brought diseases." Arcadia would not keep quiet. She continued in Tatcan: "People died. It was a time when the little birds chased the larger ones, just like now. But at first my great-great-grandmother saw nothing more than the matters of her own small life. She was newly married." Arcadia looked straight at me. "She was two years older than you are, Cesa. Fifteen years old is not too young to be married."

And Tía, almost as an echo—a French echo—said: "I was a bride at fifteen, as perhaps you will be, too, Cesa."

"Oh, no!" I burst out. "No!"

Arcadia looked at Tía; Tía turned to glance at Arcadia, almost as if they understood each other. Tía handed the pastry to Arcadia, who nodded at one of the kitchen maids. The girl carefully lifted away the little wooden door that blocked the adobe oven.

"No." I spoke loudly. I spoke in Spanish so that everybody would understand, so that my opinion would be absolutely clear. "I won't be married at fifteen, and I might not marry, ever. Look at what marriage is!" I waved my hand. "Cooking. Cleaning dishes, clothes, rooms. Over and over and over again! I am a daughter of the land! Of Madrugada! My life will always be outdoors."

64

"Cesa, you can't ride with your brothers forever." Tía returned to Spanish. In that language, she was again my stern aunt, no longer a dreaming girl.

"Cesa, the life of a woman has more adventure than you think." Arcadia also spoke Spanish; she tried to convince me. "Like the woman who discovered gold up in the Sierra Nevada." Arcadia rounded her eyes, to make her story more tantalizing. "She was with her husband and other workers when one of the men found a yellow rock." Arcadia's voice held suspense, mystery. "They thought it might be gold, but it wasn't the same color as a ten-dollar coin. So she put the rock into her soap pot, along with the lye and fat. And when the soap was ready . . ." Arcadia opened her arms in wonder. "The rock was the color of an American coin!"

"Yes. I heard about that," Tía approved.

Tía and Arcadia felt that they had won their argument. They were satisfied with themselves, with each other—with their own dull lives. I closed my eyes and wished to be anywhere else. The pace of work in the kitchen slowed. The maids returned to the tasks that they had been born to do: parboiling corn, washing vegetables. Concia dripped water through pounded manzanita berries, making cider. Arcadia supervised and Tía came to sit beside me on the kitchen bench. Warm with the heat from the oven, she fanned herself with her hand. We were all silent, all waiting for the pastry to cook. Because that is what women do: wait.

And then the little water boy ran through the outside doorway and into the kitchen. His face was a round moon of fear. *"Doña,"* he gasped, breaking our vigil. Tía frowned. "Help!" he said, and then I saw. Behind him lumbered a grizzly bear.

I froze. So did all the kitchen maids. The beast filled the doorway from jamb to jamb and more than halfway to the lintel. It moved its huge head from left to right, examining us all. Examining me.

"Doña!" Arcadia reached for the rifle that always hangs on the wall behind the table.

"Aquí!" Tía held her hands out.

The grizzly raised its nose and sniffed. With some effort it squeezed its body through the doorway and into the kitchen. It turned toward Concia.

"Santa María!" Concia unfroze and screamed.

Arcadia tossed the rifle to Tía, throwing the rifle with both hands as though it were a stick that must fly flat through the air.

The grizzly rose on its hind legs. It was taller than any man. It was certainly taller than any of us. It walked toward the sharp sweetness of Concia's cider. Its claws were as long and sharp as daggers.

Arcadia threw the powder flask, then the leather bag with the balls and patches.

The grizzly showed its teeth to Concia.

"Ay!" Concia fainted, a real faint—nothing like Hortencia's playacting.

Tía poured gunpowder, a scrap of flannel, a bullet into the rifle barrel. She rammed it all down with the rod. She stood, and Tía was a midget compared to the bear, a tiny scrap of woman. *"Oso!"* she called.

The bear looked her way, my way.

And Tía fired.

I screamed as loudly as any of the maids. The bear fell forward, missing Concia, instead squashing a basket of beans, soundly dead with a hole through its brain. Its brain, its blood, dribbled. Tía handed me the rifle so that she could shake out her skirts and smooth back her hair. She lifted her nose to sniff through the smells of dead bear and spent sulfur. "Arcadia?" she said.

"Sí, Doña Graciela." With a matching calmness, Arcadia stepped over the bear's sprawling limbs to open the oven door and inspect inside. "Your pastry is finished." Very carefully, Arcadia removed the pastry. She again stepped over the bear to set the pastry upon the table.

Tía tidied up the rifle, snapping the rod back against the barrel, closing the flask, pulling the strings of the leather bag. She, in her turn, stepped over the bear to hand everything back to Arcadia. Then Tía put her nose close to the pastry and inhaled with pleasure. "This will be our treat for supper tonight. Your grandfather will be pleased, Cesa. You may tell him that you helped."

I nodded. I couldn't yet speak. But I had to admire

Doña Graciela de Haro de Muñoz, my great-aunt. A dreamer in French, a housewife in Spanish, a killer of bears. A Californio woman.

"Boy!" Tía commanded. And the little water boy gulped back his tears. "Go find Jesús. Tell him that another bear has come into the kitchen. Tell him I want to save this skin to make a padded cover for my saddle."

Chapter 9

The River

It was Arcadia's idea to turn the tip of one of the bear's claws into a necklace. She couldn't find the servant who is most skilled in fancy carving—he had gone off to the gold mines. But she asked another servant to trim the claw down and bore a hole. Then she strung a narrow ribbon through the hole and dropped the necklace over my head.

"To help you remember," she said, "who and what you are." Which was an odd thing to say. After all, I hadn't killed the bear. But the bear claw looked, and felt, fine against my chest. I liked it.

Grego was finally released from his prison, and he was like a storm set loose upon the ranch. "To the river!" he shouted. Which is about as far as we ever go when roaming our land. Three leagues—nine American miles—and

69

I think that Grego would have run there on foot. But he didn't run; he rode with the rest of us, the younger boys and me. My ankle was so well healed that I mounted my horse without help.

We rode along the cart track. That's the path that goes from our house all the way to the de Haro landing. Boston ship captains send little boats to the landing with the goods we've ordered. Papi meets them there with the items we have to sell. Because the heavy carts loaded with hides and tallow had traveled the track only a few weeks before, the path was deeply scored.

So we went single file. We rode past grain fields where little Indian boys ran and clapped and shouted to frighten away grain-eating birds—that's their job.

"Onward!" Grego cried.

We de Haro children rode onward, through open grasslands where elk, antelope and wild horses grazed. The wild horses, especially, compete with our cattle for food, and so sometimes the vaqueros have to kill them. I looked back to see Cinco, who was trailing us all, whispering poems into the wind. Cinco, of all my brothers, is especially softhearted. He likes to ride a special pony that he has named Zoof.

"Zoof?" Grego once said. "Like the sound he makes when he farts?"

"Zoof," Cinco returned. "Like the sound of your heart when it opens to love."

That's Cinco.

The grasslands turned into forest, dense with oak

and buckeye and pine trees. We no longer saw any of our servants, any of our cattle. The track narrowed. The trees shrank to shrubs. The shrubs lost their branches, and we were surrounded by bulrushes.

Grego stopped, and we all did, behind him. The path through the marsh always changes, depending upon where there is more land and less water. I could see where the carts had sought firm ground, failed, and had to be pulled out of the mud. If we followed the shallowest cart ruts, we'd be fine.

The younger boys pulled up close behind me. Cinco began to chant:

"When I was just a baby,
I was Moses number five.
My brothers put me in the rushes
To see if I would survive."

"Oh, Cinco!" I said, over the heads and horses of Dos, Tres and Cuatro. "It wasn't really that way!"

"I would have said you, too, Cesa," Cinco returned. "But you didn't fit in my poem."

"Oh, Cinco!" said Tres.

"Oh, Cinco," said Cuatro.

It's an old story, and one that Cinco won't let us forget. When he was a baby, Mamá, Tía and Arcadia brought us to the river for a picnic. While they arranged the food, Grego and I put Cinco into one of Arcadia's tightly woven Pomo baskets to see if he would float among the bulrushes, like Moses. Which he did. Those Pomo baskets are wonderful things. Dos was old enough to understand what we were doing; Tres and Cuatro maybe not. We followed Cinco through the bulrushes until Arcadia called. Then we returned to the picnic—leaving Cinco behind, still floating, fast asleep.

Mamá was so frightened. She and Tía plunged into the water. They searched for hours while Arcadia kept the rest of us corralled. Grego and I couldn't exactly remember where we had left Cinco, and besides, he had been floating so well.

"I was lost all day," Cinco told us now, again, for the thousandth time. "Mamá didn't find me until *evening*!"

"But she did find you," I replied, as I always did. And this time I added, because it was part of the story, too: "She loved you, Cinco."

"She loved me." Cinco's voice became soft. He let go of his reins. He dropped forward so that he could wrap his arms around Zoof's neck. "I love you," he said into Zoof's arched ear.

"Onward!" Grego insisted.

We followed Grego. The bulrushes mingled with cattails; they descended to salty pickleweed. I slipped off my pony and stood at the very edge of Rancho Madrugada. Our river is called the Sacramento; it's so wide the far side seems like a foreign country. Today there were little whitecaps on the surface. Pelicans fed, plunging into the depths and scooping up fish. Herons and egrets stood in the shallows, spearing fish with their beaks.

"Let's hunt like birds!" Cuatro was inspired.

"The horses first." Tres was practical.

We unloaded our food from the saddlebags and drew lots. Dos, Tres and Cuatro had to take the horses back to a patch of dry land, to hobble them and leave them to graze. Cinco, free to play, climbed into an abandoned cart with a broken axle. Grego took off all his clothes, dropped them in a pile on the wooden dock and jumped into the water. I, more modest, kept on my chemise.

I love to swim. Mamá taught me. She once said that I swim like an otter. Which isn't true. I'm not nearly so fast and agile. But I can dive like a pelican and swim underwater like a fish. I can hold my breath for minutes—maybe. I don't really know. But in the water I feel like a fish. I feel like a bird in the air. I am something more and different than human. It's wonderful.

While Grego splashed and Cinco jumped down from the cart, I floated. The water surrounded me like an embrace. When I was ready, I turned onto my stomach and dove—down through warm, almost-fresh water to where the water was cold and salty. Down through what had been mountain snow to the ocean's long, long reach.

Our river is a mixture, a melding, a communion. That's what Padre Mournful sometimes says when he's trying to explain the mystery of Holy Communion. Which makes our Sacramento River a kind of holy sacrament, too. I put my palms together and shot up to the surface. When I reached air I felt almost rebaptized.

I looked for Cinco. Now he was playing in the shallows, trying to spear little fish with a stick.

"Cesa." Grego was treading water behind me. "Race you to the island!"

The island isn't much—just a higher piece of marsh that somehow rises above the river. It's mostly cattails, some bulrushes. Nothing else. I don't know whether it's part of Rancho Madrugada or not. But if it isn't, it's one of the few places where I ever set foot on land that's not my own.

"Cinco!" I yelled. "Shout 'Santiago'!"

"Santiago!" Cinco obliged.

We swam: Grego noisily, with lots of splashes, and I silently, swiftly. But still, somehow, Grego reached the island first. He was very proud. "You have to use my technique, Cesa. You have to swim like I do."

I didn't bother to answer. My feet squished down into mud; the mud rose between my toes. We explored what little of the island there was. We dropped off at the far end and swam back around to the front. Grego saw the men first; I didn't. Grego slowed his splashes and grabbed my arm. We both treaded water, our heads just above the surface.

Cinco sat beneath the dock, his knees pulled up against his chest and his arms wrapped around his legs. He was as small, as frightened, as a fox in hiding. Above him, two tall and bearded strangers rummaged through our clothes. Their own clothes were torn and dirty and old.

"Children!" one of the men said in English. He sounded disgusted. "We can't wear these trousers. The shoes are worthless." He turned, accidentally—or maybe purposely—knocking Grego's shoes into the water.

"The food was tasty, though," said the other man. He also spoke English.

"It was foreign stuff," the first man returned, still sounding disgusted. "Mexican stuff."

"Can we use the cart?" the second man wondered. "It might be worth something."

They left the dock to inspect the cart. "Wooden wheels?" the first man sneered. "It must have been made by Indians. I've never seen anything so primitive. Look, the wheels are nothing but slices of tree trunk."

Cinco sneezed.

It was only a little sneeze, and he held his hands tight over his nose. But the men heard, and in seconds they were beneath the dock, dragging Cinco from his den.

"Let him go!" Grego's voice sounded strange to me until I realized that he, too, was speaking in English. "I tell you, let him go!"

Grego had pulled himself back onto the island. He stood, as fierce as he could be. I clambered up beside him.

"*Señores,*" Cinco wept.

"Mexican kids," the second man said calmly. "Dirty little Mexican kids. Although that one knows how to talk."

The first man whistled, a low and disturbing sound. "A little *señorita.*"

I looked down to see that my wet chemise was almost invisible, my bear claw nestled between my small breasts. I was obviously very much a girl.

The first man leered at me. And then, amazingly, he began to sing:

> *"All the* señoritas
> *Want to learn* inglés.
> *'Kiss me!' cry the Yankees*
> *And the girls all answer, 'Yes!' "*

He made kissing sounds with his mouth.

I was more disgusted than he ever possibly could have been.

"Suéltenme, señores," Cinco begged.

"Let him go!" Grego repeated fiercely.

"Let the little greaser go," the second man told his friend, and he demonstrated by loosening his hold on Cinco's arm.

The first man raised his hands above his head in mock surrender. Cinco darted away into the bulrushes and disappeared.

"Where did you learn English?" the second man yelled over to Grego.

Grego was too furious to answer.

The first man still stared at me. I slipped back into the water, my hair floating behind me like a nun's veil.

"What's 'mermaid' in Mexican?" the first man called.

"Come on, J.R.," his friend said. "There's nothing for us here."

I think J.R. wanted to stay and tease us some more, but his friend told him, "The sooner we get to the gold fields, the richer we'll be. You can buy all the *señoritas* you want on our return. If you like this spot so much, you can come back here to farm." Which was enough to make J.R. go: up the river, away from our landing, into marshes where we rarely walk—but which are still part of Rancho Madrugada.

"*Juro por Dios!* I hope they drown in the mud!" Grego swore.

Grego swam for his shoes. I swam for the landing. As soon as I touched shore, Cinco emerged from the bulrushes. His face was still puffy and red from crying. I held him close. "You were very brave," I assured him. "Very brave indeed."

When the other boys returned from putting the horses to graze, we had to explain. We all sat in a circle on the ground, Grego and I still wet, Cinco sometimes sniffling. I put my arm around Cinco again and hugged him as tightly as he had hugged Zoof.

"They were Americans," Grego began.

"They were ugly!" Cinco squeaked. "They pulled my arms! They called me a greaser!"

"Well, they're gone now," Dos said when we finished our story.

"We must tell Papi and Tía," Tres mused.

"No!" we all said at once—or at least I, Grego, Dos and Cuatro did.

"They didn't really hurt Cinco," Grego emphasized.

"And if we do tell Tía, she may not let us come to the river anymore," I warned.

"Which means no swimming," Dos added.

Cinco still looked frightened, but the rest of us were united. "Oh, all right," Tres finally agreed.

All of my brothers swam then. Even Cinco. I led him into the water and taught him how to float. I kept my hands under his back, just as Mamá had held her hands beneath my back all those years ago. "Listen, Cinco," I said, and I sang the song that Mamá once sang to little sheep:

"Listen to me,
Come back to me,
Because I love you so."

It's a silly song, a baby song, really, and Cinco was too old for it. But he listened while I sang. He even sang it with me when we returned to shore, while we dressed. He made up another song of his own about the ugly Americans. When it was time to leave, Cinco mounted Zoof like a little vaquero.

But still, he refused to ride at the end of our procession. "I don't want to be lost, ever again," he said. So he kept his pony as close as he could to mine. All the way home.

Chapter 10

The Dennys and the Dons

Those were the ugly Americans. The next Americans that came to Rancho Madrugada arrived a few weeks later, along with the millstones and machinery that Papi had ordered.

I first saw the millwrights on a pale August morning just after dawn. Grandfather, Papi, Grego and I were out on our morning rounds. Papi led us to the little adobe house that he had allowed for the millwrights' use. It was a humble little house, one room only. These Americans were servants, not guests. But still, they seemed proud, standing in the morning fog, assessing us as we assessed them.

At first I was repelled. They looked so much like the Americans beside the river: patched trousers tucked into high boots, jackets with the shoulder seams strained and ripped, hats so dirty the original color was lost forever. There was Harry Denny with his long nose and missing teeth. His brother, Marshall, had one leg shorter than the other.

But then there was Marshall's son, Jug. I had never seen a boy like Jug before—so tall, so slender. And with eyes as blue as Jayboy's feathers! His hair was almost white and looked as soft as the fringe on Tía's best Spanish shawl. He was maybe sixteen years old, I guessed.

We de Haros, all of us high upon our horses, looked down upon the Dennys. Grandfather—in his jacket with the silver buttons, his yellow felt hat trimmed with golden braid, his spotless pantaloons and shiny boots—looked down upon the Dennys with his nostrils slightly pinched. Because these Americans were not only unkempt, they smelled.

I looked down upon Jug Denny, and I did not pinch my nose.

Papi began the introductions: "My father, Don Blas de Haro."

I waited for Marshall Denny to bow, to offer his deepest respects. But Marshall didn't even incline his head to Grandfather; he merely touched his hat. I hadn't seen all that many Americans before the war—and those that came to Rancho Madrugada were always guests—but this American was especially rude.

"Sir," said Harry, which was a little better, but not much.

They were so unmannerly, so dirty, that Grandfather spoke about them as if about cattle. "Are they sufficiently housed?"

Papi translated Grandfather's words into English. "Is the house satisfactory? You will tell me what you need—materials and labor—to build the mill. This afternoon I will take you to the spot that I have chosen for the mill site."

"Is there gold in your creek?" Harry asked.

"No." An edge appeared in Papi's voice, an edge that would have made any other of our servants become, and stay, silent. "There is not."

But: "How far away is the gold?" Harry asked.

Papi concluded the conversation with a little slap of words: "That is irrelevant." He turned his horse's head. We all moved away with him.

I don't think Grandfather understood the English, but still he remarked, "I question my wisdom, Nico, in allowing you to bring these men onto our land."

"These men and this mill are an investment for the future." The more Papi talked, the more enthusiastic he became. "The hide and tallow trade is falling off. The new economy will be based on grain. We will grow grain, we will grind flour, we will sell flour to the Americans. You will see, Father. Where we lead, all the rancheros will follow."

"Hmpf," said Grandfather.

Grego and I sped home. We gathered our little brothers in a huddle just outside the dining room door.

"They look like—" Grego suddenly fell silent because Tía passed by us. "You know, the river," he whispered when she was a few steps away. Which was enough to make everybody understand.

"*Mets-toi à table,* Cesa!" Tía ordered me to sit down in French. *"Siéntense,"* she told the boys in Spanish.

We had to sit; we had to eat our breakfasts. But Cinco kept looking at me, again and again.

"These Americans won't hurt you," I promised as soon as we were free of the dining room. "They can't. Papi brought them here. They're rude, but they're not bad."

"They could be bad," Cinco worried.

"When you see them, you'll know that they're not." I made Cinco ride with us that afternoon so that he would be reassured. Papi took us all back to the Dennys' house. I made certain that Cinco saw Jug. "Look!" Jug's eyes and hair were even prettier in the afternoon sun than they had been in the morning mist. Jug blazed; he shone. He looked *very* good.

"That boy's a *güero,*" Cinco said with suspicion. "He's as white as an egg, even his lashes. His eyes are naked."

"Just because he's blond doesn't mean that he's bad!"

Cinco shook his head.

"Oh, Cinco!" Irked, I kicked my pony away from his and went to listen to Marshall Denny speak to Papi.

"We will walk," Marshall announced in loud English.

82

"If we need a horse, we will buy it from you right and proper. We will not be beholden to you or anybody else. That is the American way."

"American way?" Cuatro was listening, too, but he didn't fully understand the English.

"They want to walk," Grego explained.

"They must ride," Tres argued. "They are our servants. They may use what is ours."

"They don't know how to ride." Dos had made up his mind about all Americans.

"Lead us on to the mill site." Marshall's American voice boomed over our Spanish ones.

Papi allowed the Americans to walk. He, on his horse, led. We children, on our horses, followed. Four of my brothers rushed ahead and then came back, like dogs that don't know exactly where they are going but want to explore. Cinco kept right by me.

Papi led the way into grasses that were high and thick, sometimes razor sharp and often barbed. We de Haros broke the way with our ponies, but still the Dennys had to push through with their hands. Their hands became welted, red. Their clothing gathered hooks and spurs. The grasses rose to Harry's waist: ruthlessly, he shoved the golden grasses aside. He peered down to their stems looking for—I think— metal gold. The grasses rose to Marshall's chest: He worked his arms while moving forward with a lift and a twist, his good leg leading and his shorter leg following. Marshall wheezed; the going was hard.

83

But when we reached the spot that Papi had chosen for the mill, Marshall seemed pleased. "Good!" he said. "Wind from the west today. Will there be wind from the north later?"

"On many days," Papi told him.

Marshall turned all the way around, as if to smell and feel every angle of the wind. He kept his eyes closed, putting all the power of his senses into his nose and skin. So he didn't see what I saw: Papi had chosen a section of Madrugada Valley where the land was high and flat and the wind rippled the grasses like waves upon the river. A place from which I could see so much: east to the rising hills; south to where the valley narrowed; west to the tree-lined creek; north to where the valley widened as the creek fell to the river.

"Ouch!" Jug's exclamation was loud. "Thistles!" His hand dropped spots of blood.

I rode up to him. I left Cinco and spoke in English, which made Jug's eyes open wide. "One reason we ride is because there are thistles in the grass," I said.

Jug smiled. He stood in the very center of Rancho Madrugada, and his smile was as bright as the day.

"I'll take you back to your house now," Papi told the Dennys.

I wanted to follow that smile. I turned, too.

"No, Cesa," Cinco protested.

I hesitated.

Grego had an idea. "There's more to find out at home." Meaning we would learn almost everything

84

there was to know about the Americans if we asked Arcadia. Arcadia's opinions are culled from all the servants on the ranch. What they know, she knows. What she thinks, everybody thinks.

Jug and his father and uncle were pushing grasses aside, this time with their hands covered by the cuffs of their sleeves.

"Cesa!" said Cinco. Grego waited, as did Dos, Tres and Cuatro. I could only see Jug's back, no longer his smile. *"Cesa!"*

"All right!" I went with my brothers.

We found Arcadia in the midst of supper preparations; she wasn't welcoming. "Out of the way," she commanded.

The boys and I drifted to different corners. When Arcadia thinks she's too busy to talk, then it's best not to ask her a direct question. So: "The Americans won't ride horses, Arcadia," Grego said, by way of prodding her into a conversation.

Arcadia's lips thinned with disapproval. We had her attention. "Those Americans think too well of themselves. They class themselves higher than the vaqueros."

"Higher than the vaqueros?" Dos was amazed.

"That's what people say. That they are arrogant. That they are dirty. That they have no useful skills." Arcadia cut away at a round of roasted beef as though she were cutting away American vanities. "And they speak a language that nobody can understand. They are too different from us; they don't belong here. We never needed a mill before. Why Don Blas listened to Don Nico and allowed him—" Arcadia caught herself and stopped before going any further; she never, ever criticized the family, at least not in our presence. "It is the will of the dons," she finished. And she put all of the beef into the stew pot, where it would sit and blend until supper.

After supper Grego grabbed my arm. "Let's go spy on the Americans," he said. "Just us, not the little boys."

I agreed, readily. Grego and I sneaked out of the house before our brothers could ask where we were going. We saddled two ponies and headed down to the creek. We crossed the creek with hardly a splash, the water was so low. We bypassed the little village of stick and mud huts—some adobe—where all our Indian servants live. All, that is, except for Arcadia and the female house servants, who share the big room next to the kitchen.

The Dennys' house was in the Californio vaqueros' village, beyond sight and sound of the Indians. But in between the two communities there's a third, a special grouping of small adobes where the Indian and half-breed vaqueros live with their families. It was from this community that Grego and I heard music, the melancholy intertwining of guitar and violin that somehow always pulls the heart out of my body. Californio music, of love and loss and longing. Of heartbreak and redemption. Of tears and joy.

The song faded away into the night. There was a pause of silence and sorrow that even the nocturnal katydids and howling coyotes seemed to respect. And then another violin—of a brighter but less rich tone—cut into the darkness with such a liveliness and merriment that the previous mood was completely shattered.

"Is it dance music?" Grego wondered, for this was a tune that neither of us had heard before.

We rode into the Indian vaqueros' village, to where a fire was lit even though the night was so warm. And along with the group of Californios and Indians that had gathered there for companionship and music, we waited. We watched with our people as the Americans approached from the Californio vaqueros' village. The Americans didn't seem to care whether or not they were welcome. It was Harry who played the violin, an American fiddle. Marshall limped with confidence. Jug was a spot of starlight until he neared the fire. Then he glowed as yellow as the sun.

"Draw back," Grego whispered, which I did. And which our Californios and Indians did, too.

Harry kept on playing. Marshall stomped his longer leg, keeping time to his brother's music. He began to sing. "Come to the West and settle and labor on free soil," sang Marshall. And then: "Our lands they are broad enough, don't feel alarm. For Uncle Sam is rich enough to give us all a farm."

"Who's his uncle Sam and what farm is he going to give away?" Grego asked. "What's he singing about?"

Grego sounded as suspicious as Cinco. But I felt no alarm. For I was gazing at Jug. I was thinking that maybe there were two kinds of Americans, ugly river Americans and young, beautiful Americans. It was easy to forgive the one kind when I was looking at the other.

Chapter II

At School with Padre Mournful

The Americans had been with us for about a week when Padre Mournful called my brothers and me to class. Our education has always been sporadic, depending upon Padre Mournful's other duties and what else is going on at the ranch. But at breakfast on this day, Padre Mournful was firm in his intentions: "School," he commanded.

We had to wait until the breakfast dishes were cleared. Then we all sat around the big table: the little boys a seat away from each other so that they couldn't nudge and cheat, Grego in Grandfather's chair at the head, I in Tía's at the other end.

"We will begin with a discussion about pride," Padre Mournful said in English. He teaches almost all subjects in English: that is Papi's directive. "Then we will examine those people who are prideful. Dos?"

Dos stood and began to form his mouth around the English language. "The sin of pride . . . is . . ." Dos thought hard. ". . . very bad for a person because it makes him sin."

I'm not certain Dos could have done any better in Spanish.

Padre Mournful pointed to Grego.

"There are two kinds of pride." Unlike Dos, Grego spoke fluently. "Deserved pride and unearned pride. Deserved pride comes from birth and situation in life. Unearned pride is an unreal estimation of who you are." Grego smiled, pridefully.

Padre Mournful nodded, ignoring Grego's smirk. Padre Mournful saw sin elsewhere: "Sinful pride now walks among us," he warned. "People who refuse to accept the truth and sacraments of the Holy Catholic Church."

He was talking about the Americans! About Marshall and Harry—and Jug. Padre Mournful didn't mention their names, but I knew.

"Prideful people have narrow, closed minds," Padre Mournful said in a tone that allowed no argument. "So I will tell you about fences. American fences. Symbolic fences—blights upon the mind. Real fences—blights upon the landscape. The younger boys will take my dictation. Cesa and Grego, you may work on your signatures. But I want you to listen."

90

We all picked up our pencils, put them to our slates. Grego and I began our assignment first. Our assignment was fun. A Californio's signature is his seal of honor. He puts it at the end of every letter, every document. It must be so unique that it can never be forged. María Francisca Octavia de Haro Vallejo y Vega—that is all of my name with all of its parts. It takes a great deal of effort to write my name properly, but the result—fancy letters, swirls and curlicues—is very beautiful.

"Californios, in their freedom of land, in their freedom of thought, have no need for fences." Padre Mournful spoke the English words slowly, clearly. "But Americans build fences wherever they go. Protestantism is a most dangerous kind of fence."

Cuatro looked up from his slate. "Padre?" he asked. "How do I spell *Protestantism*?"

I didn't know, either. But I decided that I didn't really care. I left the conversation then; I let Padre Mournful's words surround me like a meaningless haze. I glanced down the table. Grego was working on his *G*. Cinco was drawing. I squinted. Cinco was drawing a pony, probably his favorite, Zoof. He was drawing, and no doubt thinking, in Spanish. I began to embellish my *M;* I, too, began to think.

The Dennys had refused to come to the great Mass that Padre Mournful gives every year to celebrate the Assumption of the Virgin Mary. All the vaqueros, all the Indians—every other servant—gathered in our

91

western yard. Instead of horses, the corral was filled with people. We de Haros knelt on the veranda. Padre Mournful stood before a carved mahogany table and celebrated Christ's death and resurrection with all of its splendor. But the Dennys stayed away.

Swallows flew overhead during Mass. This is the time of year when they flock and fly south. Their breasts were specks of white against the summer blue sky. After Mass, everybody ate and ate, for all the women had been cooking for days. Everybody ate and then danced, and then they ate and danced again. The day deepened into night, and the falling stars of August were as numerous as swallows' breasts.

But the Americans didn't come.

I put my elbow on the table, my chin in my hand. I began to draw the head and face of a boy. A boy with a smile as bright as sunlight and hair as pale as Spanish silk.

A boy who was no doubt Protestant.

I hardly paused. I went on to draw eyes, a nose. My mind drifted into thoughts so pleasurable that I could feel my heart becoming warm. I wondered: How many hairs are there on the head of a boy as blond as a seeding dandelion? I drew strand after strand, carefully, delicately. With a tender touch. And as I drew, that warmth within my heart expanded. It exploded: *zoof!* It was almost a sound; Cinco's sound of love.

Love? Was I in love? I had never been in love before. I looked up and around. My brothers were writing, drawing. No one had heard. It was a very small *zoof*, after all—hardly a burp. I composed myself, drew all that warmth back inside my body. I hid it. I made my thoughts purely mathematical. How many hairs? That was counting, numbers. Any romantic thoughts I would have to confess to Padre Mournful.

But Padre Mournful must have heard something, somehow—priests have mysterious powers. Luckily, he heard only one word. "Mathematics." He glanced at Tres, who is his star pupil. "If one square league equals four thousand, four hundred twenty-nine acres, then how large is Rancho Madrugada in the American measurement?"

I scratched away at my slate. I scrawled numbers beneath my drawing. After all, nothing had happened. Had it?

"Rancho Madrugada is one hundred forty-six thousand, one hundred fifty-seven acres," Tres said aloud, before anybody else had come close to finishing. "Which is also two hundred twenty-eight square miles," he added unnecessarily. He almost always goes the extra step, which is why Padre Mournful likes him.

"Cesa." Now Padre Mournful stood behind me. "Have you decided to sign your letters with a drawing of a face?" He only saw a face; he didn't know that it was Jug. I laughed, weakly, along with my brothers.

"We will put your face on Cinco's horse," Padre Mournful continued, "and then maybe we will resume our lessons." Cinco's laughter stopped; now the scolding included him.

"I will read to you from the works of John Donne, an Englishman who was once a Catholic. Therefore his poetry is almost acceptable." As Padre Mournful read, Tres leaned over and very quietly translated for Cinco. I listened to Padre Mournful, then Tres, then Padre Mournful again.

"Permítame amarla," Tres whispered.

Which wasn't exactly what Padre Mournful was saying, but close. "Let me love."

And my heart opened again, this time so loudly it should have deafened the world. *Zoof!*

Chapter 12

The Doña of the Mill

"Let me love!"

That became my goal. It was all that I could think of. But I didn't tell anybody. And I *certainly* didn't confess. I kept my heart a secret.

In secret, I planned.

The day after Padre Mournful's lesson, Arcadia stood on the veranda just outside my window, blocking the light that should have come into my room. "I see a swallow chasing a hawk," she announced portentously.

I ignored her because I was dressing. I own a very lovely petticoat: The skirt is pale orange muslin, printed all over with darker orange and red leaves. The yoke at the hips is a dark orange-red satin. The waist ties with orange-red satin ribbon, and I have more of that ribbon with which to tie my hair.

I pulled the petticoat over my laciest chemise. I tucked my bear claw down inside the neckline so that it was hidden—it was the wrong kind of necklace for such finery. I tied my hair with the ribbon, and then I peered in my mirror. I was shadowy but pretty. I looked like a leaf of the autumn that was about to come.

"Well!" Arcadia had turned now to stick her head, her shoulders, her breast, into my window alcove. "So this is how things change!"

I raised my nose and sniffed—exactly like Tía. Then I danced out of my room, into the courtyard, and around to the western yard, where my brothers were waiting.

"Why are you wearing that, Cesa?" Grego asked. "I thought we'd go out to the windmill."

"Cesa isn't going. She's staying here with me." Cinco was pleased.

"I am going," I contradicted my smallest brother.

Cinco frowned.

"Well, you can't wear that on a horse." Dos sat on a corral rail as though it were a pony, one pantalooned leg on each side. "You look ridiculous!"

I kept my head very high; I pointed to the very best pony. "I will ride that roan," I said in Tía's most ordering voice.

"Do you want a sidesaddle?" Tres was incredulous. "For your petticoat?" He knew, they all knew, that for years I had been avoiding learning how to ride sidesaddle. It's such a ladylike accomplishment.

"No." That wasn't something I'd thought of. Well, I didn't have time to learn now.

My brothers were puzzled, but they obeyed: Dos saddled the roan. And I discovered that there's a reason for sidesaddles. Riding on a man's saddle in a fine petticoat is not easy. I bunched the petticoat up as I mounted, but still my foot caught and tore the flounce. Grego broke into a gallop. My skirt flapped up over my thighs; I had to hold it down with one hand. The boys pounded ahead; I had to slow my pony to a walk. Just before reaching the windmill site I had to stop, to drape the petticoat back over my legs.

Be modest and proper and wear your prettiest clothes. That's what Hortencia had said. Those were the rules for catching a man. Hortencia hadn't said how difficult those rules were to follow. I combed my hair with my fingers and retied the bow. Then I took a deep breath. When I was ready, I brought my horse up to the little gathering of de Haros and Dennys.

I smiled my loveliest smile.

Everybody ignored me.

But they were busy. Jug, his father, his uncle—they were all hard at work. Already they had scythed a large patch of grass down to the ground. Now they were drawing a huge circle within the patch, digging the outline of the shape with shovels.

Marshall stopped to lean upon his shovel, its length

almost making up for his short leg. He glanced over at us. He scowled, but not as though he was angry—as though he was thinking. "Your pa said that we could use some of those Indians. You talk American, don't you?" he asked Grego.

Grego held himself as tall as he could, a junior don upon his horse, a lord of the land. "I do," he said in a deeper voice than was his own.

"Well, we got to dig a trench for the foundation. And then I got to talk to that brick maker of yours. Does he talk American?"

"No." Grego kept his voice low.

"Who here talks American?" Marshall sounded exasperated.

For a moment I thought that Grego wouldn't respond. Marshall's tone was too insubordinate, Grego's superiority too high; they didn't match. But: "I do," Grego finally allowed.

"We'll need someone to talk to the Indians, the brick maker, the carpenter," Marshall listed.

"I can do that," Grego assented.

So this is how things change: At that moment, on that day, Grego became something new—Don Grego of the Mill. Every morning thereafter he rode out to the mill site to confer with Marshall about Marshall's needs for the day. Then Grego began his rounds. "We will need eight thousand bricks," he told the adobe maker, "and maybe more later on." Grego was suddenly important—like a short and bossy Grandfather.

98

He rode around the ranch ordering and directing, pretending that the orders were his alone, not translations from Marshall. He even called the Dennys "my men." Meanwhile, I dressed. Every morning, after riding with Grandfather, I came to the breakfast table wearing what was clean of my prettiest clothes. I didn't want my family to know exactly what I was doing, but I did want them to see me. Tía raised her eyebrows; she never said a word. Padre Mournful didn't, either, although sometimes I sensed that he was holding his tongue with both hands. Or maybe somebody else was holding his tongue for him. Papi was the only one who said anything, and what he said was perfect. "You look like your mother," he told me.

Those words made me feel so special, so very pretty. I floated out to the corral, as beautiful as I could ever be. I looked like Mamá. In so many ways I *was* Mamá. Maybe.

Cinco frowned at me. He was always frowning at me nowadays.

"Oh, Cesa," said Tres.

"I look like Mamá," I told them. And then I said something else: an exaggeration, maybe a very small lie. But something that I had to say if I didn't want them to tease me, to become five boys against one girl. "Mamá always rode astride."

Now they couldn't say anything, out of respect for Mamá. Of course Mamá never lied. But sometimes a lie is necessary. Really.

So with no teasing, without comments, unhindered, I rode astride every day out to the mill site. My petticoat modestly draped, I watched Jug.

He never returned my gaze. But he was so very busy. All of the Dennys were excellent workers, very good servants. They worked from dawn to dusk. They walked back and forth so often from their little adobe house to the mill site that they created their own path. "Shank's mare," Marshall told Grego one day, which I didn't understand until I listened further. "Shank's mare" means traveling on foot. "I can walk a good long while on my two legs. Which is what honest Americans do, and which is what God intended." And then Marshall looked at Grego's horse with something almost akin to scorn.

Pride! American pride! Denny pride, too, I suppose. But Jug wasn't prideful. I could tell that by the way he moved. So beautifully. He did everything his father asked. Sometimes Jug would begin to glance my way and I would feel my heart start to trill. He never met my eyes, though. Reluctantly, my heart settled down.

That didn't mean I was discouraged. I continued watching. And waiting. And listening. Jug rarely spoke. But Harry talked, always. And always about gold.

"When we've finished the mill, you may go up to the mines," Marshall told his brother. "But until then, we have a contract. Nico de Haro paid our passage; we will build his mill."

Gold. Harry wasn't the only one of our servants

with that obsession. Grego—who now always dressed formally, in a waistcoat and jacket and almost-clean shirt—sometimes stopped his pony next to mine. "Two more Indians have left, Cesa. And another vaquero went to Papi and said that he was sorry, but he had to try his hand at the mines." Grego shook his head, the slow shake of a man whose mind is full of important thoughts. "It's a shame, but Grandfather says that our people will soon return to their senses, return to Rancho Madrugada."

In my opinion, it was Grego who had lost his senses, pretending to be something he was not. An adult. Don Grego. But then . . . had I lost my senses, too, waiting so long for Jug to look back at me? What were the other rules for getting a man's attention? I had probably slept through Hortencia's most important advice! Then, one morning, Tres joined me at the mill site.

Dos, Tres and Cuatro had long since tired of the mill. They rarely stopped by. So Tres was surprised by the progress: What had once been a deep, round trench was now a foundation for a round brick tower. Brick by brick the tower was growing—as tall as a buckeye tree, taller. When Tres arrived my head was tilted backward. Jug was high above me, his long legs and round rear framed by a ladder, his white head as bright as an angel against the blue sky.

"Here." Tres had brought a basket of end-of-summer huckleberries. I looked down from heaven and picked out the berries that were mottled with white bloom. I ate those first; they are always the sweetest.

"How are they doing it?" Tres asked. He saw with different eyes than I. "How do they measure?" And then he did what I should have thought of doing, what maybe I would have thought of doing if I hadn't been thinking like Hortencia. He asked Jug.

Jug looked at his father for permission. Marshall nodded. Jug came down from the tower, long leg after long leg. "All of our measurements depend upon the circumference we choose," he said. "Horizontal and vertical. We use this." He showed Tres a rope that was knotted at intervals.

"How do you determine the angles?" Tres asked. Which was a question only Tres would think of. Padre Mournful would have been pleased.

They had talked long enough about numbers. Jug and I had more important information to share. I leaned over my horse's neck and whispered—because somehow that was the loudest my voice would come—"Why do they call you Jug?"

Jug glanced at me, glanced away, then glanced back. Did he like me? Did he not like me? What did those glances mean? But all he said was, "It was Ma's idea."

I held his eyes. I was now beyond any rules; what was bold for Hortencia wasn't bold for me. "Is it your real name?"

"Why, yes." He didn't look away.

"Like a jug that people pour water from? How do you spell it?" I persisted.

Jug colored—white-haired boys can blush fiercely. "I wouldn't know."

"Jug!" his father commanded, and Jug had to climb back up the tower. But first, he smiled.

Zoof! My heart thrilled with ecstasy. He had smiled! He couldn't write, but he could calculate numbers in his head faster than I could with all of Padre Mournful's teaching. He was amazing!

The season changed, and I sat happy upon my horse. I relived our conversation again and again. Then, on an afternoon when the leaves of the wild grapevines down by the creek were almost the colors of my autumn petticoat, Grandfather came to the mill to observe. He looked up to where the Dennys were setting a ring of smooth, rounded timber upon the tower's open rim.

I studied Grandfather while he studied the tower. Grandfather looked suddenly small. Which was a silly thought. Of course he was smaller than a tree-high tower. But still I felt unsettled about something.

Grandfather turned his horse, then stopped it so that he could observe me. He observed me just as he had observed the tower: not as if I were a girl dressed in orange who looked like her mother, but as if I were something foolish. As foolish as an American mill on California soil. He shook his head. "Oh, Cesa." He didn't say anything more. He rode away.

I stared after him. Oh, Cesa? I wasn't foolish! I could prove it. I had a very real, very special relationship. I rode up to the height of adobe brick. "Jug!" I called.

"Is it that girl again?" Marshall's voice came from around the far side of the tower; I couldn't see him. He spoke as if he didn't believe that I understood English. "Tell her to back away from the mill. She's a lazy one. These Mexicans are a shiftless people."

He sounded exactly like the Americans beside the river. But the Dennys were different—*Jug* was different.

"Jug," I called again, this time with demand in my voice. I wanted him to say something back to his father, to defend my honor and that of all Californios. To speak the truth about what he and I meant to each other.

But he didn't. He didn't even glance down at me. He just let some clay drop my way.

Clay? And suddenly I was furious. That American boy had *feet* of clay! I shook my petticoat so that the clay flew and my skirt flared bright orange. It was a vibrant flame—a Californio's strong light. Not the wispy white-blond gleam of American cowardice.

I backed up my pony. If I'd had something to throw, I would have. Instead I turned and rode swiftly away. My bear claw bounced a little beneath my chemise. It touched my heart, the same heart that had trilled and *zoof*ed and been so happy. It had been a false happiness; now I knew. Now I realized the truth: He had never liked me. Not at all.

The next day I kept on my pantaloons. After second breakfast I rode far away from the mill. I rode with Cinco, who once again smiled at me. We rode high into the hills of Rancho Madrugada. We watched monarch butterflies fly past on their way to their winter roost beside the distant ocean. We saw squirrels chase each other from oak tree to oak tree, excited by the annual ripening of acorns. I saw all those wonders, and I waited for them to soothe my heart. But they didn't, not completely.

The days passed. With birds that migrated overhead. With leaves that fell. With the sound of wind shifting, autumn shifting, from west to south to west again. And then the time came when Marshall announced that the mill roof and sail frames were completed, that the mill was ready for operation, that he would show us all how it worked.

I think everybody from Rancho Madrugada came out to the mill that afternoon. People and horses ringed the mill site. Some of the vaqueros' wives brought picnics. Grego stood proudly before the mill door, wearing his best waistcoat with the ivory buttons. Papi shouted out to our people how far away they should stand. What they could expect to see and hear.

Marshall unfurled the canvas sail covers; Harry and Jug pushed upon a great pole and turned the tower's roof into the wind. Jug's back was lean and strong. I didn't want to notice, but I did. The sails caught the air, they creaked, they spun.

"Ah!" It was one gasp from four hundred people. Papi and Grego smiled at each other, don to don. The Dennys looked at each other and nodded, Denny to Denny. Inside the mill the great stones turned. Two Indians poured wheat into a hopper. Everybody at Rancho Madrugada ate mill-ground wheat flour that night.

"Metate-ground flour is better," Arcadia said. I couldn't taste the difference.

"Our new mill is a step forward, into the future!" That was Papi talking.

"Bah," said Grandfather.

I avoided the mill site. I avoided all the places where I thought the Dennys might be. But I had to return to the mill once. Because of Grego. Because in one great action he lost his title of don. He had been a man's man for weeks. But the day after the sails turned, Grego left off his waistcoat and jacket and rode out to the mill site. With me and the little boys watching, he climbed up a moving sail. He clung to it like a spider to a web, and all the while the sails turned as if Grego had no more weight than a spider. Around and around, upside down. The little boys shouted and laughed. I laughed and wondered if Grego would fall on his head and die.

But he didn't. He didn't even break an arm or leg. He just dropped off the sail as it turned toward earth; he collapsed upon the ground as dizzy as a spun top.

106

He looked up at us, clustered around him, waiting to see if and when he would return to his senses.

"You try it, Cesa," he finally said. "It's fun!"

But I wouldn't. And not because the sails were so tall, or because they moved so swiftly, or because I was afraid—I wasn't. But because I didn't want to be foolish again.

Mrs. Denny's Pies

Papi wanted the Dennys to stay with us forever and run the mill. But that wasn't what they wanted to do. So they left. First, though, in appreciation and as a reward, Papi gave them an embroidered purse filled with silver coins. Marshall took out three of the coins and returned them to Papi in exchange for a horse.

"Why didn't he just *take* a horse?" Grego asked me. We stood in our western yard watching these transactions. Papi was smiling, generous. Marshall was reserved, as formal as a person can be in a ripped jacket and dirty hat.

I couldn't answer Grego, because I didn't know. We have so many horses—and many more that are wild on our ranch—that we often give horses away to the occasional travelers who pass by. We give horses and food and clothing, whatever is needed. I had never seen a horse bought for money.

The sorrel pony that Marshall selected waited patiently while Jug and Harry heaved sacks of flour onto its back. The Dennys went on foot—traveling away by shank's mare—leaving behind only one reminder of their stay: Papi's mill.

An Indian family now ran the mill. I think every child on the ranch at least tried to ride the sails—and a few broke their limbs. Jesús was kept busy mending what the wind and American ingenuity broke. Then Grandfather issued an order: Nobody but the mill Indians was to touch the sails.

Grandfather was pleased that the Dennys were gone. He didn't say so, but he seemed more relaxed when we rode out on our morning rounds. More relaxed than he had been for months. Once he even made a joke.

Those were the first days after the Dennys left.

Then Gaspár came to our house and stood in the parlor before Grandfather, Papi and Uncle Isidro. And Grego and me, who were there, too. *"Señores,"* Gaspár said, ignoring me and Grego, "another three vaqueros and ten Indians have left Rancho Madrugada for the gold mines."

"They didn't come to me?" said Papi, surprised. "To tell me? To ask my permission?"

"*Señor*, they are ashamed," Gaspár said. "They know that the more who leave, the more difficult it will become to run the ranch properly."

Grego and I went outside to tell our brothers. "It's a serious problem," I explained, so that even Cinco would understand. "Without enough vaqueros, our cattle will wander too far and maybe hurt themselves. We might lose them."

"I can help. Papi should ask me." Dos twirled an old lariat in the air. "I can do the work of three vaqueros." Which was only half of a lie; Dos is indeed a good horseman.

We all laughed at Dos's boast. But that day marked the end of Grandfather's softened mood. The weeks passed by; the line of concern between Grandfather's eyes became etched deeper and deeper.

And then Gaspár came to the parlor with other news: "There are boats on the Sacramento River, boats of all sizes—filled with Americans going to the mountains, eager for gold. One of our Indians says that yesterday afternoon he saw twelve boats."

Twelve boats! So rarely did even one boat pass by our landing: maybe one boat a month, if that. "Let's go see!" said Grego. I agreed. So did Dos, Tres and Cuatro. Only Cinco was reluctant.

"We won't leave you alone for an *instant*," I promised.

This time when we went to the river, we followed the

110

creek. It's down by the creek that you see most of autumn at Rancho Madrugada. The maple and sycamore trees flash and burn color before their leaves fall. The poison oak turns as red as blood. Away from the creek it's still summer, with the oak trees looking tired and dusty after the long months without rain. But beside the creek, there is change.

The creek joined the cart track as we entered the forest. Squirrels threw acorns down to hit our heads and horses. My brothers laughed and hooted. I listened to the forest sounds, to the sounds of boys, and then I heard the call of a deeper, older voice.

"Sammy!" it yelled. "Haw!"

Cinco rode around Tres and Cuatro so that his pony was right beside mine.

Up ahead, the track opened into a clearing, where our Indians often stop with the heavy hide and tallow carts to rest before continuing onward. The clearing is perhaps as large as an American acre. The creek bed widens and flattens there, so that animals don't have to step steeply down to water.

On this day there was a little camp in the clearing: a canvas tent and an American wagon with spoked wheels. Sammy was an ox. The man beside the wagon was ugly and dirty and rough-looking.

"Cesa," said Cinco, worried.

But the man only glanced our way. He had no interest in us. He reached into the wagon to lift out a barrel as large as his chest. "Good!" a woman's voice said in English. "My lard."

She walked out from the tent, followed by a boy. *Jug Denny.* What was he doing back at Rancho Madrugada! Why was he here?

Jug showed no emotion, no reaction at seeing me. After a quick glance, he pretended none of us existed. The woman pointed, and Jug went to help the man at the wagon. The woman came up to us.

She was blond, like Jug, but much older. She wore a funny hat made of soft cloth that stuck out over her face and tied beneath her chin. Her petticoat was of undyed cotton, kept only a little bit clean by a very stained apron. "Six boys," she said. "One with long hair. Do you speakee English?"

"Yes, madam." Grego was as polite as if she had been the queen of America. Which she wasn't.

The woman's eyes moved swiftly up and down each one of us, assessing us all, stopping at the bear claw around my neck. "Mexican?" she asked.

"Californio," Grego corrected.

"Is that one a girl?"

"I am," I confirmed.

The woman smiled. "Well, honey," she said, "welcome to Denny's Inn."

"In what?" Cuatro asked, but in Spanish.

Jug and the man lifted this and that from the wagon, putting it here and there as the woman ordered. They didn't speak. The woman spoke. She talked incessantly:

"It's a wonderful place, San Francisco. Such excitement in the air! I never saw so many people in such a hurry. Hurrying for gold! And leaving all these good things on the docks to rot. Dried peaches from Chile, one man said. I tell you, when I came around the Horn it was so cold I couldn't believe peaches would ever grow in that benighted climate."

I watched Jug as he worked. He was paler than the woman. Colorless, even. He looked bleached—like a *güero*. Suddenly, I was amazed by myself: How could I have ever thought him handsome?

The woman talked on: "I had to travel behind my husband. A month behind. Stuffed into a ship's cabin with five other women. 'Ladies,' two of them. Ha! Up to no good, say I. But I try not to judge: There's enough opportunity here for us all. Although it's not what I expected. There was no news of gold when I left Massachusetts. But I can see the future; I know what it holds."

"Cesa!" Cinco whispered, calling my attention away from the woman, from Jug. "Look!"

I looked.

Somebody—not one of us, not one of our people— had made another path through the forest, enlarging what had probably been a deer trail. Now the path was wide enough for an American wagon; it led west and east, away from Madrugada Creek, making our clearing a kind of crossroads. An American road, crossing our Californio one. It should *not* have been there.

"Grego!" I said through my teeth. I kicked my pony, hard. I had never been up that trail before, but I knew where it must go: up a slope that becomes a hill that becomes a series of hills leading to the bluffs over the Sacramento River.

My brothers followed. The forest thinned with altitude. The road shrank, becoming nothing more than a narrow track that almost disappeared into the high, summer-dry grasses of an upland meadow. This American road was nothing to worry about; it was too meager to matter.

But there was something up there that did matter. A dozen or so of our cattle grazed in the meadow, searching for the tender fodder that is almost impossible to find this time of year, wandering far from home. Wandering where they should not have been. "Grego!" I called. Because we should have seen a vaquero: roping, herding. Moving the cattle back toward the center of Rancho Madrugada.

"I can do it!" Dos immediately kicked his pony and began maneuvering the cattle almost with the skill of an adult. It was a game, I think, for Dos. But for Grego, who joined him, it wasn't.

"Take the little boys back home," Grego shouted over his shoulder. "If you get there before we do, tell Gaspár."

I nodded and decided upon the easiest, fastest route back. I took my youngest brothers down to the clearing, to the cart track. Only the adults were in the camp, the

114

man leaning against the wagon and smoking a pipe, the woman bent over a fire, scraping coals away from the flame with a stick, setting a skillet over the coals.

"Fire," said Tres, and he halted us all. He brought his horse forward until he was equally distant between the man and the woman.

"So I thought," said the woman, "that our best bet—"

"Madam." I hadn't realized it before, but Tres can be just as grave and formal as Grego is when he's pretending to be Grandfather. "Please take care of your fire," Tres requested. "A stray ember will catch easily, and at this time of year fire spreads quickly."

"Why!" The woman was pleased. "You talk American, too. Marshall!" This last call was as loud as her voice could be. She brought her tones back down to a more reasonable listening level. "You must be the children that my husband described." The woman nodded at the silent man, but not as if he were her husband, more as if he were a stranger whom she chose to instruct. "Dark as pickaninnies, all of them, and heathens of the Roman faith. Their people haven't yet invented the wheel, but they manage some English." She bestowed smiles upon my brothers as if she herself had taught them the language.

"Madam," Tres began again, and this time his voice was especially stern, as if he would start a lecture.

But he was interrupted by Marshall Denny, who came into the clearing from the eastern side of the new path, carrying a hatchet. Marshall walked with the familiar lift and twist of his shorter leg. "Some nice land back there, Mrs. Denny," he said. Marshall crooked his eyebrows when he saw us—as if *we* were the people who didn't belong in the clearing.

"Firewood, meat. What more do I need?" Mrs. Denny answered her own question. "Fruit," she decided. "I need fruit." She turned to Cuatro, who was the de Haro nearest to her. "Do you have fruit to sell?"

Cuatro—as spun around by her onslaught of speech as if he had been riding the sails—took an apple from his pocket and handed it over. Even his hands looked dizzy.

Mrs. Denny examined the apple and again nodded, this time briskly. "Marshall!" she called, as loudly as before, even though her husband was well within hearing. "Give me a half dime."

Marshall dropped a coin into his wife's hand.

"You, girl!" This time Mrs. Denny chose me. The coin passed from her hand into mine. "Take this back to your mother. It should be good for . . . I would say five bushels of fruit. Bring me the first bushel tomorrow."

"Let's go," Cinco begged.

We went.

We burst upon Tía in the parlor, where she was dusting. We all spoke at once.

"The cattle are almost all the way to the river!"

"Marshall Denny has a wife, and he's brought her back here!"

"They're camping on our land!"

116

Tía heard us all together, and separately, too. She divided our words as though they were different kinds of beans stirred up in one basket. She made sense out of what we were saying. And then she asked the question that none of us had yet thought of: "How long do the Dennys plan to stay there?"

Cinco wouldn't return to the clearing. But the next day the rest of us did, Grego, Dos, Tres, Cuatro and I. We brought Mrs. Denny her apples, and we observed: even with the addition of a makeshift table of boards and stones, the camp was still very rough, uncomfortable. Not permanent. Just big enough for the three Dennys.

The pipe-smoking man and his ox were gone. The wheels from his heavy wagon had left ruts in the softer earth beside Madrugada Creek, widening the American crossroad. "He went east, to the gold mines," Tres said quietly, in Spanish.

"Oh, children!" Mrs. Denny chided. "Talk American, now. It's the only language that God understands. It's time to lose your heathen ways."

"Heathen?" said Tres, again in Spanish. He rolled his eyes upward, to God.

But Mrs. Denny had moved onto another subject: pies. "In Massachusetts we lived near a turnpike. I sold pies and coffee. But I know that I can charge more here. Much more. Where else will the men eat? What you give, you lose. What you sell, you increase." She turned to me. "Girl! Can you cook?"

"No," I answered.

"Pity. You might have been useful." Mrs. Denny continued to think out loud: "Fruit pies for one dollar, meat pies for two, coffee for twenty-five cents a glass. Coffee mixed with this and that. Venison mince. They will sell."

The next day, the day after that—for several days—my brothers and I returned to the clearing. Each time we expected to find it empty. But the Dennys lingered; only Harry Denny, apparently, had been in a rush to go to the gold mines. Once we found Marshall standing in the middle of our creek—by autumn the water flow isn't even ankle-high. Marshall frowned at Grego and said, "I like my own mill to be a water mill, but not if these droughts are persistent."

These Americans made no sense at all.

But then the day came when we found something very different at the clearing, something startling—two wagons and four men stopped beside Mrs. Denny's canvas tent. Three of the men sat at her table on log stumps; the fourth stood. They were all eating hand-sized pastries, two or three to a man. Mrs. Denny walked among them, smiling, talking and pouring a dark liquid from a kettle into cups and mugs. Sometimes she took money from the men and put it into her apron pocket. Nailed upon a tree there was a large wooden sign with the words Denny's Inn roughly lettered in charcoal.

"In what, Cesa?" Cuatro said, frustrated.

Tres tried to explain. "Not *in,* but *inn.* Remember Don Quixote? Remember the story about the inn?"

I let Tres answer. I watched as though the clearing were a stage and the Americans actors. Not real, but very real. An American play. On *our* stage.

I felt my temper rise in my throat. Didn't the Americans know that they were trespassing? That they were eating their pies and drinking their coffee on the soil of Rancho Madrugada? Without our permission?

The men at the table were rough, maybe dangerous, but I had to speak. I began to translate my thoughts into English. But before I could say a single word, another horse rode up behind our group of five.

"Cesa!" said Tía's voice, and she most definitely meant "stop." My brothers and I all turned to see Tía riding upon her bearskin-covered sidesaddle.

Tía examined the men, the sign, Mrs. Denny at her fire.

"Twenty-five dollars today alone!" Mrs. Denny lifted more small pies from her skillet. "This is a country where gold comes in more than one color!" She looked up, saw Tía and continued. "Some of the apples had worms, but I don't mind. And the men don't, either. Worms cook just as well as fruit. Waste not, want not! Would you like to buy some pies, ma'am?"

"Cesa." Tía's voice was very cold, very commanding. "You will come home with me."

Chapter 14

Uncle Sam Is Rich Enough

Our lives changed overnight.

From then on Tía kept me at home dusting, making beds, beating carpets. She assigned the real housemaids to the orchards for the fruit harvest; she turned their chores over to me. "I need your help," she said. While Tía consulted with Arcadia in the kitchen, deciding what our meals would be for the next day, I worked with Arcadia's one remaining kitchen maid cleaning vegetables and chopping fruit. I missed my rides, my days outside. But also—strangely—I didn't. Not always. With so many of our servants elsewhere, there was a frenzy in the house that carried me along. I had become another woman of dawn with two strong hands.

My life changed. And so did my brothers'. Because

Gaspár needed more riders, Dos was given his dream and promoted to junior vaquero. He and Grego left at first light with Papi and Uncle Isidro—who were now emergency vaqueros, too—and only returned late at night. When they did come home they were almost too tired to speak, too tired to tell me how far they had had to track the cattle, what problems they had found in the herd.

That meant I had nobody to talk to except for Tía. And in our hours of working together she sometimes conversed almost as if I were an adult.

"The Dennys must leave," she once mused, "of their own accord. That would be the best resolution. Better that they leave on their own than that they be forced to go."

She and I were putting Grandfather's room in order. Grandfather's canopy bed is bigger than mine, much finer, with carved rosewood posts. And higher. To change the sheets, to pull up the blankets, I had to stand on a stool.

"We will pray for it, Cesa. The Dennys must leave." Tía handed me a pillow.

"The Dennys must leave," I echoed. *"Absolutely."*

Tía chuckled at my vehemence. "Even Jug?" she asked.

I know that my face colored.

"Oh, Cesa," said Tía. "I watched you, I saw you. I knew how you felt. But I also knew that your affection wouldn't stay with Jug. That it would return to us, the ranch. In so many ways you remind me of your mother. She was loyal, too."

I stopped working; I needed to hear more. "Loyal?" I repeated.

"Loyal to even the smallest creature on Rancho Madrugada. Once there was a hummingbird that lived in the big pine tree just outside the kitchen door. During nesting season, every year, your mother put bowls of sugar water—our precious sugar, boiled into a syrup, for a bird!—outside on the bench. One year she forgot. The hummingbird buzzed around her head until she begged its pardon—'Perdóname,' she said—and set out a bowl. She never forgot again."

Tía laughed at the memory. I laughed with my great-aunt, wishing so much that I could remember what she had known. Tía's tones became more serious. "Your mother always said that this land, the creatures on it, came second only to her family." Tía reached up to touch my bear claw. "I taught your mother how to shoot a rifle. To protect herself, to protect the ranch. Back then we were often long days without men."

Tía left to begin work in another room. But I remained to settle the pillows onto Grandfather's bed, to tidy his clothes. "Loyal," I whispered to myself. "Mamá was loyal."

Thinking about Mamá, the hummingbird, made my chores easier to bear in this time when we, too, lived long days without men. At noontime even Padre

Mournful rarely came to our table, having so many duties elsewhere. Sometimes, though, Grandfather joined us. Every day that he could, Grandfather rode out with Papi and Uncle Isidro and Grego and Dos. But often his back would hurt or his legs would ache and he would stay at home. Then Grandfather came to the table smelling of unguent—Jesús uses the same unguent for muscle pains in horses and people.

"Let the Americans have their gold; we have our land," Grandfather once muttered.

It was dinnertime. I was wriggling, trying to get my legs up on my chair so that I could sit tailor fashion, away from Majo's teeth and claws. Majo was meaner than usual. His battles with Jayboy were fiercer than ever—Jayboy once drew blood.

Grandfather said nothing more. But he looked so old and worn. And angry. Angry because our huge herds of cattle—twenty thousand head—were roaming as far as our most distant boundaries. Angry because our vaqueros continued to leave us.

On All Saints' Day, when Padre Mournful said Mass in the western yard, I saw for myself how few vaqueros remained. Only seventy, maybe eighty, knelt on the hard-packed earth, their heads bowed. Only half the number that Rancho Madrugada needs.

But even these men slipped away—by ones, by twos, by dozens. Ashamed, they left at night, taking nothing but their saddles and horses, taking nothing but their hopes to the gold mines.

Grandfather, Papi, Uncle Isidro, Grego and Dos—by necessity their life became our cattle. The mill Indians disappeared, and now I spent hours in the kitchen grinding corn by hand. Only Tres and Cuatro still roamed our ranch, and they began a habit of reporting to me. "There are new Americans almost every day at Mrs. Denny's inn," said Tres. On this day I was sweeping the veranda.

"She shows no signs of leaving," Cuatro added.

"She's selling baskets made by our Indian women," Tres continued. "She gives them ribbons and beads and buttons, and they give her baskets. She sells the baskets to the Americans for five dollars each—and they pay it."

"Five dollars!" It was an amazing amount. "Why do they need baskets?" I asked.

Concia, who had once been a kitchen maid and was now mending clothes, sat on the veranda, avoiding my broom. She took pins and scissors from her sewing basket of deer grass. The little water boy sped by, picked up Concia's basket and shook it, just to annoy her. "Panning for gold," he teased.

So I knew.

My brothers rode off. They made it their job to observe the Americans. They had become spies. They skulked around the edges of the clearing, eavesdropping on conversations. Because they were Mexican boys, the Americans acted as if my brothers were invisible.

"There are *ten* of them!" Tres exclaimed on another afternoon. "And when I say ten, I'm not even counting the Dennys!"

The boys always made their reports to me in the late afternoon. That gave me all day to wait for them. And ponder. While I swept and dusted I tried to see what they saw: our clearing, so crowded now with trespassers on their way to the mountains.

"They killed one of our cows!" On this day, Tres was angry. "They are thieves: greedy and wasteful. They only ate what they needed for one meal, and then they left the hide too ripped up for anybody to use! They're shooting antelope and elk. They shoot everything!" Tres worked to compose himself. "But they'll soon pass through and be gone."

"Except those that are staying," Cuatro remarked. Tres and I both frowned, and Cuatro stammered a little, flustered by our scrutiny. "Al-Although the Americans that are staying might be the same ones who are coming back from the gold mines. I'm not sure."

"Coming back from the mines?" I had thought the Americans were only traveling in one direction.

"You need to study more English," Tres chided Cuatro. "You couldn't have understood properly. The Americans are all going east, and none are stopping to stay."

Tres was right, Cuatro was wrong. But still, I

couldn't help dreading: What if some Americans were discouraged? What if they weren't finding gold at the mines? What if they really were coming back, wanting to stop and maybe stay? Like Mrs. Denny.

I had too much time to think, too much time to imagine, too much time to worry. I began to envy my older brothers: Their worries—our cattle—were right before their eyes. And the boys were making a difference—that's what Papi said. He said that Dos was becoming a better horseman every day. Grego was once so exhausted he fell asleep during supper. But even so, Grego somehow sparkled. He was doing real work now; he was important, not just pretending. And even I had to admit that he was taller.

Meanwhile, I had only one creature to tend: Cinco. Cinco spent most of his days following me about, keeping within range of my voice and eye. He drew letters in the fine, dry dust of the western yard. He crept up on slow-moving tarantulas, making them jump like crickets. He waited, patiently, for the tarweed to open its late-afternoon flowers. And all the while, Cinco made up poems:

"An autumn flower is a thing to see.
It smiles at Cesa, it smiles at me."

The fact of an autumn flower was nothing new to us, but it was something that excited the Americans.

126

That's what Tres said. "They talk about farming," he reported. "They sit around Mrs. Denny's table and say this drought year has to be unusual and next year the land should yield two crops."

I tried to puzzle that one out.

"They don't know it's dry like this every year," Cuatro contributed.

"They say it isn't American to own as much land as we do," Tres continued. "They say no family needs more than one hundred sixty acres."

One hundred sixty acres. I did a quick calculation in my head, but Tres beat me to it: "Rancho Madrugada is almost one thousand times that size."

How could one thousand families live on Rancho Madrugada? That's an absolute impossibility. We don't have enough water. Those Americans were crazy!

But still, I tried to think like them while I went about my housework. I tried to think like someone who can't tell the difference between rain clouds and fog. Like someone who doesn't know our seasons. Like someone who won't believe that one cow needs five acres for feed.

And then, one day, Cuatro mentioned Uncle Sam.

"They say that Rancho Madrugada belongs to Uncle Sam," he said. "Who's that?"

I knew because Uncle Isidro had told me. "Uncle Sam is the government of the United States of America," I said. And I shivered in the sunlight of our western yard. Because now I understood our danger.

"Well," said Cuatro, "he doesn't own our land."

"Well," said Tres, "we lost the war."

Padre Mournful has sometimes preached that there are virtues in solitude, that retreat from society enhances prayer. And that prayer can protect what you love. During the following days I did something that was as strange to me as sweeping and grinding corn: I prayed. I prayed for hours on end. I hardly talked; I ignored Cinco's songs. Instead, while my hands worked, I concentrated on the land that I know so well—the vernal pools of spring, the first hot dust of summer, the ground squirrels that live at the edge of the chaparral, the wild grapes that are almost too tart to eat. I saw our cattle, our people, the creek that gives life to us all. And the great river that is our boundary. *Our* boundary, the boundary of the de Haro family. The boundary of Rancho Madrugada. I filled my soul with all that living land. And then Tres came home in a tear, Cuatro close behind him, their ponies heaving.

"They're building a fence," Tres gasped. "They say that our land is theirs! They call themselves homesteaders."

There's a time to pray, and then there's a time to take action. To muster forces. I ran into the house, to Tía's room, to tell her. Tía was also praying, on the velvet-covered kneeler that is her prie-dieu. She listened very carefully. She questioned Tres and Cuatro.

Then she opened her wardrobe, took out a scarf and tied it securely over her hair.

"Cesa!" she said, and for once Tía didn't mean "stop." She was as strong and commanding as any Californio general ever was during the recent great war. "Tell Jesús to saddle our horses!"

Chapter 15

The Fence

We weren't a very threatening army as we rode out: a woman, a girl, an old Californio servant, a priest, and two little boys. Tía rode sidesaddle upon her bearskin pad. Padre Mournful rode astride with his robe hitched up so that his legs hung bare. Jesús rode as if he had been sewn to the saddle from birth. And then there were me and Tres and Cuatro. Cinco wouldn't come.

We rode two leagues, the adults talking and planning, the little boys anxious and angry. I was angry, too, of course—and very worried. But I was also enjoying my first ride away from the house in what seemed like forever. The grasslands were more beige than gold now, both on the hills and in the valley. They always turn brown, bleached by summer, in the last month before the rains come. The chaparral was dusted to gray. The coyote brush still bloomed—little white flowers that dotted the gray and brown like white specks in rough-woven wool. Like the specks in Padre Mournful's undyed everyday robe.

I let my horse lag behind the others. I put my nose up into the air, closed my eyes, and smelled. Soon the world would turn from dry to wet. From sun to rain. The grasslands knew. The oak trees knew. The chaparral knew. They were waiting.

Because we traveled so far and our ranch is so large, the fence looked very small at first sight. Tres shouted, "There!" and pointed. I only saw a line and three or four tiny dots. The homesteaders had chosen a spot right in the center of the widest part of our valley.

The fence grew bigger and bigger. I saw that three men had finished a side and a corner, that a fourth man worked behind the fence hitting a length of wood with an ax.

"They cut down that oak tree," said Cuatro.

The American fence was nothing like our Californio fences. Until now the only fence on our land had been the corral: branches of large trees and trunks of narrow trees that were laid on their sides, one atop the other, and held in place by shorter stubs of oak. This American fence was both more purposeful and stern. The board lengths between the hewn posts made tight triangles of air. It wasn't a fence just to keep things in, but to keep things out, too. Us.

Tía said something to Padre Mournful and he rode forward. The men stopped in their work, curious but cautious. One, then all, tipped their hats in Tía's direction.

"My good men," Padre Mournful began.

One of the Americans cracked a smile.

"Perhaps you do not understand the situation here," Padre Mournful continued.

"A man or a woman?" the smiling American said to his friends. It wasn't a nice smile. "Or something in between?"

Padre Mournful took a deep breath. He dismounted, giving his reins to Jesús. He stepped toward the fence and the rest of us rode up, just a little, so that we could hear.

"I am a priest and a friend of the de Haro family, whose land this is."

"Oh, no." The smiling American shook his head; he seemed to be having fun. "This is American property here."

"This is El Rancho del Valle de la Madrugada." Padre Mournful spoke excellent Spanish, then perfect English. "Owned, by legal grant, by the de Haro family."

Two of the Americans looked at each other. I thought their faces were just a little unsure. But the smiling American stepped closer to Padre Mournful. "A Mexican grant," he scoffed. "Not valid anymore!"

The unsure Americans stepped closer, too.

The man with the ax joined his friends. They became a fence in front of the fence: a fence of men. "I heard a brigadier general in San Francisco say we won

132

California, fair and square, in the war. So this is America now. American soil. And in America, all unoccupied soil is free for the taking."

"A brigadier general!" One of the other men nodded, all of his uncertainties now gone.

Padre Mournful took another deep breath. "But this land is not unoccupied. As I said before, it is—"

The smiling man interrupted. "Do you see a house, Carl? Do you see a barn? Do you see a fence?"

"No, sir!" said the man named Carl, and he turned a full circle, facing hills and valley and the brown edge of the marshlands and the evergreen line of the forest, until he turned back to us again.

"And that, Mr. Woman, is proof that this land is unoccupied," the smiling man said definitively.

If I hadn't been there, on the spot, with my eyes on Padre Mournful, I wouldn't have believed what happened next. Padre Mournful took three long strides, so quickly that his robe flowed behind his body as if pushed by the wind. He lifted his right arm until his wide sleeve fell back almost to his shoulder. And with one swift movement he punched the smiling man's nose.

The smiling man screamed in pain. Blood spurted out of his face and over Padre Mournful's fist. Two of the men grabbed Padre Mournful; the third jumped back over the fence and ran for his ax.

"Yip, yip!" Tres cried. He and Cuatro were off their horses and running into the fight.

I was half off my horse when I heard a familiar hiss in the air, the angry sound of a lariat. Jesús was wielding his rawhide rope as though it were a very long whip. He drew welts on the faces, necks, arms and hands of the smiling man's friends. The ax man tried to grab the lariat; his hands were now as bloody as the smiling man's nose.

"Home!" Tía shouted.

And I added the more military sound, "Retreat!"

Which we did. Jesús's lariat was so many places at once, it was like an angry swarm of wasps. The Americans could do nothing but try to protect themselves. Padre Mournful pulled up his robe and jumped on his horse. "Yip, yip," cried Tres as he, too, mounted.

The last to leave the ground was Cuatro. He was small—the lariat whizzed far above his head. But he was fierce. He aimed one last kick at the smiling man's shins. "Greaser!" Cuatro snarled.

Tía led the retreat. Jesús remained long enough to keep the Americans confounded; then he followed us at a gallop. By the time he caught up, we had slowed our horses. The fence was again just a line—with some angry dots—behind us.

"What did they say?" Tía asked Padre Mournful. Neither she nor Jesús had understood more than one or two words.

But Padre Mournful was too anguished to answer. "A sin against charity!" he said again and again. "A sin against charity! A Cistercian does not fight. I am worse than a Jesuit!"

"I wish I could hit that hard," Cuatro said enviously.

"Enough!" Tía's voice cut through all personal concerns. "We have a great problem."

We rode back home. There was nothing we could do or decide until our men returned. We had the rest of the afternoon in which to wait and worry. I stayed on my horse, riding out by myself after the others had gone inside. I crossed over the creek, which was the barest trickle now. Madrugada Creek never completely dies, but by the end of the dry season it's so slender that even Cuatro can jump it. My horse's hooves clattered; the clay banks were as hard as fired pottery.

I rode into the settlement where our Indian servants live. It looked like a normal day, with the women at their fires, cooking, and the children playing. "Where is Tomás the adobe maker?" I asked. "Where is Fausto the carpenter?" I asked after every man whose name I could remember, and I always got the same answer.

"He has gone to the gold mines, *señorita*."

I rode to the village in between, where the vaqueros who are not quite Californio live.

"He has gone to the gold mines, *señorita*."

The adobe cottages of the Californio vaqueros are larger, sturdier. They and their families cultivate small patches of land within our ranch. Normally, the vegetable harvest would be over, the squashes and pumpkins cut and put into storage. But now some of the gardens were untended, the pumpkins turning to mush.

"He has gone to the gold mines, *señorita,* and I don't know what we would do if it weren't for your great-aunt. She has ordered everyone who is able to work in the de Haro gardens and orchards—even your house servants, even the holy priest. And then we share the produce at the end of the day. We work together; nobody goes hungry. God bless Doña Graciela!"

Mothers were worried that their children might go hungry! How could I not have known? What had I failed to see?

I rode back to the creek and crossed over to the orchards and gardens that supply our table. My brothers and I rarely spend time there. We are interested in climbing the hills, speeding across the valley; we have never been interested in pulling carrots or picking apples. We have never thought much about food.

The apples were mostly picked now. The pumpkin stems had neat edges from which the fruit had been cut. The Indians toiling in the gardens looked cared for and fed. The *zanjero*—the toothless old man who opens and closes off the irrigation channels with little boards—sat beside a channel and mumbled into the wind. He was thin but not starving.

I stopped beside him. "There is little water," I remarked to myself as much as to him.

The *zanjero* opened his mouth into a smile of pink gums. I had to listen hard to understand. "But there is rain on the wind."

When I returned to my own home, I spent a long minute gazing at the wide yard, the veranda upon which sometimes a dozen people rested, the great whitewashed adobe. Our house is so many times larger than any other house on the ranch. We de Haros are responsible for the lives of so many people.

I corralled my pony myself, put away the saddle without help. I walked up onto the veranda, through the parlor, into the courtyard, into the kitchen. I couldn't find Tía, so I spoke to Arcadia. "There's nobody to bring home the sheep this year," I told her. "Our people will need the wool for clothes. So I will take a group of women up to the mountains after the rains come."

Arcadia's busy hands stopped; she studied my face. Then she put down the dough that she was slapping into tortillas. She put her hands back together, but this time open and flat with only the smallest fingers touching: a platform on which to balance a globe. "It is women's caring that holds up the world," she said.

Chapter 16

Fuego

Grandfather, Papi, Uncle Isidro and my two oldest brothers didn't come home until late, well after dark. They were very weary. We ate our supper in silence, for it was Grandfather's order that we discuss nothing until the table was cleared. When we finally moved into the parlor I went to stand behind Tía. Grego sat in a chair that was as close to Grandfather as Papi's and Uncle Isidro's chairs. Dos, like a vaquero who wasn't quite a Californio, sat on the floor between the men and us women.

"I regret, Don Blas—" began Padre Mournful.

Grandfather waved his hand. "What is done is done. And there was provocation."

"We must approach them from a legal standpoint," Papi stated. "With proof of our land grant."

I saw with my mind: In Grandfather's room there is a special chest that contains both a simple map of our boundaries and three long and beautiful scrolls. The handwriting on the scrolls is done with flourish. The official signature of Governor José Figueroa gives Rancho Madrugada formally to us.

But Uncle Isidro was cautious. "That may not be enough, Nico. American courts often insist upon surveys and titles—surveys done by Americans and titles granted by their authorities."

"None of that matters." Grandfather had already made up his mind. "We will convince *these* Americans with force."

Uncle Isidro shook his head: "I would not advise that, sir. The political situation throughout California is uncertain, delicate. We must move slowly, and with great caution."

But Grandfather's decision ruled. And the next morning we rode out again—all of us except for Cinco and Padre Mournful, who was mourning his lapse from charity. Grandfather, Papi and Uncle Isidro were our vanguard. Gaspár led a group of vaqueros, only twenty in all. Jesús rode ahead of a small army of Indians, again only twenty or so. Tía and I, Dos and the children rode at the very end, like a tail. Tía was as much a warrior as anybody. The rest of us had refused to stay at home.

We were all armed, the men with rifles and handguns. Grego rode behind Gaspár and wore a real sword. Tía carried the kitchen rifle. The smaller boys and I carried wooden clubs. We were armed but under orders to restrain our violence—at first. After hours of discussion Grandfather had reluctantly agreed to moderate his plan. First Papi would speak peacefully to the Americans. Papi would attempt to convince, to parley. Once he failed, we were free to fight. Although the children and I had to speed back home the moment that Tía said we must.

Riding at the tail of the army, I worried. I knew something about fighting, if only from games. "We need a strategy, tactics, maneuvers."

But instead we rode with clatter, with determination, with bits and pieces of the army straying away now and again to check on cattle. The Indians sang; I understood most of the words.

> *"An arrow against a moon-shield,*
> *Splits it all apart.*
> *Little birds go flying,*
> *Aiming for your heart."*

It went something like that.

Tres was listening, too. "Change," he said. "Cesa, do you hear? They're singing about change."

"No." Tres wasn't translating the same as I was. "They're singing about battle. About fighting the enemy."

We passed through herds of cattle until, finally, I saw

140

the fence. Today it was much bigger and more massive than a simple line. And today it was surrounded by dots, many dots, making little black clumps near the fence and then separating to go behind it. Dos, whose eyes are better than mine, told me what he saw: "Wagons, lots of wagons." And as we got closer: "Wagons with American wheels."

I don't know how many wagons there were—perhaps as many as a dozen. They were lined up like a barricade in front of the fence. I couldn't see all the men because many were hidden by the wagons and others kept running from place to place. But I counted more Americans than there were de Haro troops. More Americans, and every single one held a rifle ready to use.

"Where did they all come from?" Dos asked.

"Mrs. Denny's inn," Cuatro replied.

I thought I saw Marshall Denny back behind a wagon. I know that Jug was protecting the fence; his hair made him so very recognizable.

Papi bravely rode forward. All the American rifles swung toward him like needles on a compass. I wanted to tell our Indians to move to the left, our vaqueros to move to the right. To prepare to attack. But instead I sat quietly at the very back of all the action, straining to hear.

"I am Don Nicolás de Haro," Papi began, "and this is my land."

This is my land. Only four words, but they hold so

much. *Zoof!* And my heart exploded with love for Rancho Madrugada. This was a true love—so much greater than anything I had ever felt for a white-haired boy. An enemy.

This is my land. To the Americans those words were a challenge, a gauntlet thrown to the ground. The Americans didn't talk with us, they didn't argue. They certainly didn't parley. Instead, one of the men shot into the air and then lowered his rifle at Papi.

Beside me, Tía unstrapped her rifle from her sidesaddle. I gripped my club and did not prepare to speed home.

Papi backed his horse, then turned it so that he could confer with Grandfather and Uncle Isidro. They were three men talking together, the horses upon which they sat making a three-pointed star. They were three men between two armies of rifles, as now all of our men were aiming at the Americans.

"Cross fire!" I exclaimed.

I was worried about Papi, Grandfather, and Uncle Isidro. My attention was on them, so I didn't see the Americans working busily between two of the wagons. I didn't notice them moving aside the cut boughs of trees. Because I didn't see it, I wasn't surprised by the sight of a long nozzle mounted between two large wheels and pointed toward us. I—who had once thought myself a real general, of sorts—lost track of the enemy. Which is the biggest mistake that you can make during war.

Boom! It was a blast to break our ears. Not just because it was loud, but because it was so unexpected. Papi's horse shied; Gaspár shouted at his vaqueros to pull back; Cuatro's horse tried to bolt, but he held it, valiantly. Other horses and riders were struggling. And while I looked to see what and where and how, the Americans cheered and laughed.

It was a cannon, small but deadly. And now the Americans were putting another ball into the muzzle, they were preparing to fire another round. Their first hadn't caused any harm—I don't know if the Americans or the cannon itself deserved the blame for the poor aim—but Grandfather lifted his hand and everybody, all of us, pulled back out of range of cannon and rifles. Now the Americans jeered at us from a distance.

"Cesa?" said Tres.

I couldn't speak—it was all so impossible!

Now Gaspár and Jesús conferred with Grandfather. One of the Indians, a chief, joined the group. We at the back couldn't hear what they said, but even I could see the fury on Grandfather's face, the gritty determination of Papi. Uncle Isidro looked almost calm, but I had seen that look before—it was the look he had when a grizzly bear was advancing and he knew that either he or it would die.

"Kill the bear!" I heard Cuatro's voice rise high and shrill. "Kill the ugly bear!"

But the bear killed us, or tried to. And in doing so it wounded itself. Because the Americans fired their cannon again, and this time they set fire to the grass. The dry, dry grass that the cattle munched on without enthusiasm. The land of tinder that was waiting for rain.

I don't know if the spark dropped from the muzzle or flew with the cannonball. But we heard the *Boom* and looked to see where the ball had fallen, again harmlessly; we looked away reassured. And then one of the Indians said, *"Fuego."*

Fuego. Fire. It starts so small, it seems so harmless. Just a little puff of smoke, a little flame of gold. And then, like a storm, it's everywhere. There's nothing hungrier than a fire in California. It eats grasses, trees, chaparral. It chases little animals from their hiding places; it terrifies larger animals so that they run mad, endangering themselves and each other.

"Hombres!" Gaspár yelled. The vaqueros broke away from our army and rode into another kind of action, herding and grouping and driving our cattle away from the racing flames.

The Indians surrounded Tía and me and my two little brothers. "Down to the creek, *doña*," said an elder. "Down to the creek."

The Americans were running, too. But most were on foot; few had horses. They left their wagons and fence and cannon to burn. If the wind blows from behind you—as it was blowing at the Americans—it can be impossible to outrun a California fire.

I was herded like a human longhorn. I smelled the smoke, heard the gleeful laughter of the fire. I looked

144

behind me whenever I could. I knew what I would see because I had seen it before: the bare and utter blackness of land consumed by flames. Death upon the earth.

"On, *señorita*!" an Indian urged.

We rode to the creek, crossed over, and took the cart track back to our house. Arcadia had filled her wait with energy, and there was food and drink for everybody. But we and the Indians ate only a little, until Grandfather and Jesús came home.

"The fire has already burned a square league," said Jesús. "It will continue to burn until there is rain."

I filled a plate with food and took it to Grandfather. He sat on his chair in the parlor, his back so straight he might have been receiving petitioners who wanted him to allow this or that. He was as straight as a king—or a soldier. And like a man of eminence, he wept. Not wispy tears, or tears of self-inflicted fury, such as I have often shed. But the rolling tears of anger and defeat that leave the eyes and fall unheeded to the chin.

" 'Our inheritance is turned to strangers, our houses to aliens,' " said Grandfather.

Which is a quote from the Bible, I think.

Chapter 17

The San Judás Tadeo

That night it rained. Gentle drops at first, that pinged one by one on the roof tiles. I got out of my canopy bed—I hadn't been sleeping—and climbed into my window alcove to see. And hear. And smell. And pray. I prayed to Mamá, who isn't a true saint but maybe, really, ought to be.

I wasn't the only member of our household who kept vigil with the rain. Tía stood on the veranda holding a lantern. In its light I saw the dust in our western yard jump like crickets. One drop, two drops. And then a deluge. I inhaled blessed moisture into my lungs and sighed. Part of my prayers were answered; now the vaqueros could come home.

They came home to the light of Tía's lantern, an hour or so before dawn. I jumped down from my alcove, onto the veranda, and went to help them put their horses into the corral. The men, the horses, were drenched and exhausted. My brothers were only shadows and sounds. "We found Marshall Denny," Grego told me. "He couldn't outrun the fire."

I tried to imagine, then stopped myself from seeing. Beside me, Dos retched at the memory: the sight, the smell, of a burning death.

We all went to bed and slept for maybe a minute. And then: "Light of the sky! God's gift to mankind!" Tía's voice rose to rejoice in a new beginning, as she did every day, for every possibility. Other voices joined in: Padre Mournful's, Arcadia's. Papi's voice, determined to praise. Uncle Isidro's voice, as angry as fire. I listened for Grandfather's voice but didn't hear it. The little water boy's song rose in a treble.

My oldest brothers slept through music and first light. They joined us in the dining room for breakfast. Dos's eyes shifted, always moving, never staying, as if he had to see but didn't want to, ever again. Grego's eyes were steady. He glanced my way and I smiled. I smiled at the new furrow in the center of Grego's forehead, at the weary darkness beneath his eyes. I nodded, as one equal nods to another. I was proud of my brother *número uno*, Grego, El Único.

"We are fortunate that none of us shot an American," Uncle Isidro remarked. "That would have brought an inquiry, and one of us might have been hanged."

147

"For defending our land?" Grego asked.

"For killing an American," Uncle Isidro answered. "This is America now."

"But there is hope," Papi spoke out.

"There is not." Grandfather's voice was harsh.

"There may be hope," Uncle Isidro cautioned. "The treaty that closed the war supports the concept of our rights. But American sentiment does not. We must be prepared to lose some—maybe much—of our land."

Grandfather said nothing more. His face closed in on itself as if he wished to hide his feelings. He didn't discuss Papi's idea to appease the Americans, to offer a white flag; he didn't discuss hard-hitting and tough legal strategies with Uncle Isidro; he answered none of my brothers' questions. When he finally stood, Tía rushed to his side.

Grandfather had never needed help before—and I don't know if he really needed help then—but Tía took his arm and put her cheek against his shoulder. "Brother," she said, and her voice was almost unimaginably gentle, "remember: We are always smaller than history."

Smaller than history. In the days that followed it seemed to be the small things that mattered the most. The wooden sail frames on Papi's mill broke in the wind. Uncle Isidro rode away to Los Angeles, in search of an honest American to survey our land. Majo and Jayboy had a great battle somewhere out of our sight. We knew of it only when Cinco, crying, carried Jayboy's broken body onto the veranda.

Tía examined Jayboy and then shook her head. "I'm sorry," she told us. She stepped out into the rain-soaked yard: "Majo, *mi guapo!*" she called. My handsome one.

I saw and heard nothing at first, then a tiny dragging sound from behind the manzanita. Majo, who had hidden himself to die, pulled his body toward Tía's voice. She knelt in the mud to run her hands over his blood-matted fur. *"Mi guapo,"* she said again, softly. *"Te guardaré en mi memoria."* I will remember you forever.

So I learned that even at the end of things there is always something left to love.

During the days of Uncle Isidro's absence, Grandfather stayed within the house. Papi, my oldest brothers, Jesús, Gaspár and the vaqueros—they were working hard to move all the cattle away from the Sacramento River and American hands. But Grandfather never joined them. He just sat upon his chair in the parlor, the chair that nobody else ever dares to sit in. He spoke very little. He looked out the windows. He scowled at the days of dryness, he scowled at the days of rain.

And the rain continued to fall, off and on, heavy and soft, as it does every year. It fell on our courtyard, the western yard, the orchards, the gardens—all of Rancho Madrugada. Soon the hills would be green. "Soon I can bring home the sheep," I told Tía.

"We will wait," she said.

So we waited. And the rain continued to fall. On us

and our servants. On the Americans, too. As before, it was Tres and Cuatro who brought the news back home.

"Mrs. Denny is offering beds at her inn as well as pies," said Tres. "There are seven tents in the clearing now."

"They've built a new fence, just at the edge of the burnt land," said Cuatro. "They're building a wooden house."

"Harry Denny has returned from the mines and is raising a mill in the clearing, beside the creek."

"Their carts and wagons have turned the path into a road."

"I heard one of them say that they'll name their town after Marshall, Dennyville."

At long last, Uncle Isidro returned home. He brought with him a surveyor who carried brass instruments and wooden poles and a chain as long as our house. Uncle Isidro showed the surveyor the map that until now had satisfied everybody's questions about our boundaries. The surveyor shook his head. "No," he said. "The courts won't accept this. It's too Mexican: only a sketch with landmarks."

Uncle Isidro told us that the surveyor was an honest American, but Grandfather turned his face away. He turned his back on the man the one time they chanced to meet in our western yard. Grandfather waited until the surveyor had been set to work, with an extra pony to carry his tools and Jesús to show him the way. He waited until the American was far from our house. And then: "You have done this without my permission," Grandfather said to his sons.

"It's for the best, sir." Uncle Isidro's reply was respectful.

"It's for the future," Papi said stoutly.

"We also must decide," Uncle Isidro continued. He had spoken to many people in Los Angeles, Americans and Mexicans both. He had conferred with an American judge. "We must choose." Soon the first year of the peace treaty would be over; we Californios must choose our future nationalities.

"If we become American," Papi told us, "we can fight for our land with their tools. Their courts, their lawyers, their judges."

"If we remain Mexican," Tía returned, "we will stay closer to who we are."

My brothers debated the question back and forth. All except for Cinco, who didn't fully understand, and Cuatro, who was absolutely stubborn about not becoming American. "I kick their knees!" Cuatro said fiercely. "I kick their groins! I kick their heads!"

Grandfather made no threats, but his voice was as fierce as Cuatro's: "I will never cede *anything* to those people."

"We may decide as a family," said Uncle Isidro. "Or we may decide as individuals."

I listened to everybody's arguments, to everybody's talk. Then I took a pony out into the mist. I rode up into the hills, over the bleak, sodden grasses. I searched

151

for the vernal pool but couldn't find it; it's only a shallow settling of land this time of year. But I knew where it almost might be, and that's where I halted. The rain started up again, plastering my hair to my neck, pasting my eyelashes to my cheeks. I turned my head back, opened my mouth, and drank. Drank of the sky, the clouds. I slipped off the pony, removed my shoes, and stood rooted in the soil of Rancho Madrugada. My mother's land. My motherland. Again I drank, as though I were a plant preparing to grow. A live oak, a sagebrush, a poppy. "I am a Californio woman," I told the sky. "I am me."

Back home, Uncle Isidro was penning an official list. "Nico and I will become American," he announced. "Tía, you and the children will remain Mexican. Don Blas"—Uncle Isidro bowed his head in Grandfather's direction—"will remain Mexican."

That bow was a gesture of great politeness, of utter respect—but something was missing. I narrowed my eyes and considered. Grandfather didn't return the bow, which was normal. Uncle Isidro returned to his list, which was normal, too. But then I saw: Always before, Grandfather's power at Rancho Madrugada had been absolute. Now, though, it was my father and uncle who were making the decisions.

Uncle Isidro decided to consult a judge in San Francisco. Papi decided to have the mill's sails repaired. Together they decided that, if they must, they would give up for lost the northernmost leagues of

152

our land. Uncle Isidro sent a messenger to instruct the surveyor to establish our southern boundaries first. "We'll bring the sheep back along the southern route this year," Papi said to Tía.

Which was a good plan, I thought.

But then Grandfather stood from his chair. "My sons," he said, and he was speaking to all of us, not just to Papi and Uncle Isidro, "you have chosen to wage war with words, not guns. Meanwhile a bear eats us alive: fingers, then hands, then arms."

Grandfather stood like a soldier, like the king he once had been. "And so I have decided. I cede to you, my sons, that which I will not cede to the Americans: all of my land. El Rancho del Valle de la Madrugada. It is yours. To hold on to with God's blessing. To lose—or give away—with God's curse. I give you neither blessing nor curse, my children, but only a warning: We have not just lost a war, we have lost our souls."

And the very next morning Grandfather rode away, leaving Rancho Madrugada forever. He rode away without looking back. He rode away with one attendant following.

Me.

It was Tía who said I must go. "Our ranch has become too dangerous a place for a young girl to be." As if she herself weren't a warrior. As if she herself didn't know how to fight.

"No!" I protested.

153

"It is your duty, foremost and always, to take care of your grandfather."

"Oh!" If only she had not said that! If only she had given me a small reason, an insignificant reason, something against which I could argue. But she said the one thing I could not argue against. It is indeed my duty to attend Grandfather, because I was born a de Haro, because I am now a Californio woman. In this last year I have learned something so wonderful, so awful. Love, loyalty, duty: They are all the same thing.

I wept. I wept for long hours. I helped Tía pack my bag. "I'll send a trunkful of belongings after you," she promised.

And then she sent me away with Grandfather to Monterey, which is where we waited for a ship. This ship, the ship that I stand upon now.

The *San Judás Tadeo*.

Chapter 18

Listen, Wind!

Listen, Wind! Do you hear me?

Are you listening with all your gusts and blows and turns and twists? You are so salty and sticky, so damp and strange. You're not the same wind that I've known all my life, the wind I used to speak to back on Rancho Madrugada. Then I could speak Spanish. But now I don't think you understand. It's as if the ships that pass us, going north, carry the new language of the whole world: English. So I speak to you in that language, even though it makes my mind sore. So very sore. I have been talking to you for so long. But there is more to my story. Listen, Wind!

The morning that Grandfather left Rancho Madrugada I followed dutifully, purposefully, miserably.

Grandfather didn't speak to me once. We stopped for the night at El Rancho de la Plata, where Hortencia lives with her family. Hortencia spoke—nonstop. She was as excited to see me as if we'd always been friends. "I'm going to marry Major John Allgood," she said as we lay together upon her bed—which does *not* have a canopy. "Do you remember him? Didn't you once see him? He's so handsome! John is up at the gold mines. Someday he will be very, very wealthy!" Hortencia laughed.

And I hated her, almost.

Grandfather, when he spoke to our hosts the following morning, foresaw nothing but bleakness: "I will sail to Mazatlán," he said. "God willing that the storms don't take me. And then inland to Guadalajara, where I have friends whom I haven't heard from in decades. My final destination is Mexico City. I have relatives there whom I do not know. Perhaps they will welcome me."

Welcome me. Welcome us. Tía's plans for me are far more specific: I am to become a boarding student at the Convent of Saint Genevieve, where she was once such a happy pupil. I will speak French and study music, dance and painting. I will learn to bake pastries. I will make friends with the Mexico City relatives; I will make sure that Grandfather has a home. The nuns, Tía says, will help me. God willing.

Hortencia gushed her goodbye: "Oh, Cesa, will I ever see you again?"

My heart was so tight that I answered meanly. Perhaps there's something that's the opposite of a *zoof*. A *fooz* instead, when the heart closes in on itself, getting smaller and smaller until it dies of unhappiness. "I hope not," I told Hortencia, which wasn't entirely the truth. But which was the *fooz* thing to say.

For the rest of our journey to the port of Monterey I was totally alone. Grandfather was so separate—in his heart, in his mind, in his speech. It was I who had to welcome, comfort, and calm Concia—the Indian girl that Tía sent with my trunk, and who is going to Mexico City with us to be my maid. With my arm around her I helped Concia board this ship. My feet weren't any steadier.

But it's been two days now and I can walk, and sway, on this deck. My stomach is almost calm, even if these seas are not. Grandfather stays below in his cabin, grieving. Concia remains in the cabin that we two share, vomiting into a pail. It isn't pleasant down there.

So I stand here at this railing. I have no place else to go. Like Grandfather, I am in the middle of nowhere—in my body and also my soul. I am forsaken.

Go ahead and gust, Wind!

Gust from the left, where the forbidden line of land is low and dark. Gust from the right, where the un-known horizon is golden and red. Behind this ship, seagulls follow. And whales, also traveling south. The whales are large and solid, comfortable in all this water. The young whales nudge their mothers. The mothers lead the way, guiding their children without words. Oh, how I wish I had such a mother.

"Mamá!" I call that word so loudly. The wind drowns my voice; nobody can hear.

Why am I clutching my bear claw so hard? I've pricked my hand. I lick the blood from my palm. I close my eyes, just for a moment. And in that moment I see: Rancho Madrugada. Now, after months of rain, the old grasses have been washed to gray; the new grasses are rising green. The hills are turning as bright as emerald hope. The trees spread their branches with joy. Madrugada Creek is swollen so wide, it is impassable—on these days we are isolated from our Indians and vaqueros, and they from us. We worry about each other, but we worry most about the little children, who must not swim in the rushing water. Everywhere plants, like children, drink and stretch and bud and bloom.

Unlike those whose hearts have turned to *fooz*. This morning when I asked Grandfather how he was, he only muttered at me: "The Americans are a fire that will burn California forever."

Grandfather has forgotten. He doesn't remember. After a dry season, there is always rain. The fire that the Americans started with their cannon wasn't the first on our land. Other fires have started before, in other ways. And always, with the rains, a miracle happens: Beneath and around the dead and ruined chaparral rise the most amazingly beautiful flowers. Tulips and wind poppies and flame poppies, whispering bells and suncups. These are flowers that grow *only* after a burn. *Only* in a land once dead. You never see them otherwise.

With my eyes closed I can see those flowers now. They are a promise: that the land will regrow, that even after a disaster life continues, that wonders abound.

This is something that my mother taught me.

Wind! Do you hear me? Give me your force! Take that great *fooz* in my heart and turn it inside out! Push it back to front! Open my heart again to love! *Zoof!*

Because whatever else happens to me, I know who and what I am. My mother's child. A daughter of Madrugada. A Californio woman. Like the land I love, I, too, will thrive.

I will find my own wonders: somewhere.

A Historical Note

In 1845 California was a remote land inhabited by very few people: 7,300 Californios, 14,000 Indians, and 680 "foreigners," of whom many if not most were Americans. Claimed by Mexico, this territory was ruled by the dons, men of substance and power like the fictional Don Blas de Haro.

When war was declared against the United States, the dons fought. But they—and all of Mexico—lost. Mexico had to give up half of its land to the United States, including Upper California.

Meanwhile, just a month before the treaty ending the war was signed, a carpenter working in the Sierra Nevada discovered gold. The word spread, first gradually, and then like wildfire. By the summer of 1848 an

English-language newspaper in San Francisco was reporting, "Every seaport as far south as San Diego, and every interior town, and nearly every rancho . . . has become suddenly drained of human beings." The gold rush was on.

Americans were now the masters of California, and California was gold, both mineral and land. The Americans arrived by sea and from across the prairies. By 1849 the population had jumped to 100,000, by 1852 to 250,000.

The Californios were outnumbered and overpowered. Their Upper California became the thirty-first American state. A land act was passed, making it even more difficult for the Californios to hold on to their property. The ranchos were eaten away, bite by bite—by squatters, by the "law," and by the Californios' newfound poverty.

Land was all that the dons had left of any value. In an effort to save it, they sold it off, piece by piece, to raise money to pay American lawyers for "representation" in American courts. The representation failed; the dons lost even more of their land. They were caught in a vicious circle.

Some decided to move back to Mexico. But it wasn't a large migration. For most people, after generations in California, Mexico was no longer home.

So the Californios stayed, and they struggled. And they suffered the same disaster that the ancestors of their Native American servants had faced during the early years of Spanish exploration and settlement. Like the Indians before them, the Californios became a people dispossessed.

Now, as I write, it's more than 150 years later. And California has become an amazing place that the Californios could never have imagined. It's the most populous state in the nation, with people who represent the entire world.

Take me, for example. I think I grew up as a fairly typical California girl—with one Mexican grandmother, one mostly Irish grandmother, Jewish first cousins, and a German-speaking aunt from the Free City of Danzig. One of my nieces was born in Hong Kong; another niece and nephew were born in Thailand.

We're a modern family: the new California. But we walk where the old dons used to walk; we see their legacy everywhere. We hike along the trails in the Rancho San Antonio Open Space Preserve. We live in towns named Santa Cruz and Santa Barbara. We travel, some of us daily, to San Francisco. Where there just happens to be—an inspiration to fiction—a street called De Haro.

About the Author

Frances M. Wood grew up as a California girl of the twentieth century, with one Mexican grandmother and one mostly Irish grandmother. She came by her citizenship the easy way—she was born in the U.S.A. But one of her Mexican-born uncles gained citizenship only when his name was added to a bill voted into law by the U.S. Congress.

Frances M. Wood holds degrees from both Stanford University and the University of California at Berkeley. Her first novel, *Becoming Rosemary,* was named a best children's book of the year by Bank Street College and was praised by *Kirkus Reviews* as "a nearly flawless, always charming coming-of-age tale."